The Randy Scuffle Papers

Phil Reebius

The Randy Scuffle Papers

For school or book-club quantities and other inquiries, contact:
inquiries@feralpuppetpress.com

This is a work of fiction. Any similarity to persons living or dead
is purely coincidental and unintended.

All content by the author.

ISBN: 978-0-9910875-2-5

*For information about banning this book in your community, contact
a member of the clergy or your local government. They know how to
get important things done.*

For Krista, the only star in my sky:

There is no way this project would have been possible without your absolute, unquestioning support. For 22 years you have listened to all of my crazy stories. You have read and edited everything countless times, offered smart, hilarious suggestions, and you have always understood. You eagerly served as the art director for the cover photograph. You hand selected each terra-dog for uniform skin tone, and posed each one carefully in the nesting material that we gleefully bought at the same store that sells foam doll heads. From the first time we met we knew we were from the same planet. How did I get so lucky? I will never forget the look of joy on your face as you danced, unable to contain yourself, while I opened my birthday present: Clown Shoes! And so, with all my heart, I dedicate *"The Randy Scuffle Papers"* to you Krista. You are the love of my life.

Special thanks to Gary Bourgeois and Gabby Goodstein for inspiration and support. Thank you Sheila Johnson for your wonderful eye and editorial skills. Thanks to all varieties of lunch meats that await the opportunity to fulfill their destiny in brown paper bags in cloakrooms of grade schools everywhere. (Mothers, don't ever send your kids to school with liverwurst and bananas.)

Extra special thanks to Jaime and Lizet Flores for the opportunity to preview *The Randy Scuffle Papers* during the Tamale Hut Cafe Reading series, and to Bernard Cox and Jenny Seay for enthusiastically coordinating this series.

To each of you who have had the opportunity to hear some of this in previews, thank you for the encouragement and positive response to this effort!

Dr. Anderson,

Thanks for agreeing to see me. I know I come to you recommended as a person you can probably help. I hope too that you have a specialty in one of the problems that get in my head, and that is specifically the problem of things getting in my head. Like songs. But not whole songs or even part songs. They are redundant snippets of my head-music that I can't identify. Not even English all the time either! The melodies are weird and I hear other instruments all the time too like lots of oboes and tubas as exclamation points. I am not a composer. I am distracted by all the noise. It's not like when my normal theme runs in my head either. That's okay because it's my normal theme.

These are unwanted non-English non-musical songs that have their own punctuation and metaphors. The worst is when someone else is singing them, like someone I can't stand as a singer but whose voice you hear so much you want to kick their voice-box across the room! Madonna™ does that for me and I know she does it for other people too. I have the *Brady Bunch* song in my head sometimes; you know, the one where Greg sings like a frog after the Peppermint Trolley Company™ was made available to the industry? Then I start laughing right in the middle of a meeting with executives who think I am mature enough to covet bass-boats and a weird colored sweater. They don't know I can't golf, and I don't float very well either.

What bugs me is I start wondering what music they have in their heads and I'm sure I can't really share my music with them because it would stun them like when I had that accident with the baseball. So can we set up a time to come in and talk about these things? And I want to know if it's normal too. At another session we can talk about my Bea Arthur dream if it's okay with you!

Randy Scuffle
Chicago

Dr. Anderson,

Some guys were here yesterday measuring for something. I couldn't understand them at all. My mom hasn't walked in front of the window all day so I don't even know if she's home. I can only see part of her bedroom wall and mostly the ceiling, so she has to be real close to the window in order for me to see her like when she's kissing me "goodnight" through it. Then all the world can see, which is embarrassing.

The glass is starting to look pretty bad from the lipstick and fingerprints. When my mom says she's ashamed of me, I wish she could get a better look inside of my mind! Then maybe she'd get it. By the way, if she ever says anything like that just tell her I'm the product of *her* parenting efforts, and I'm not as dumb as she thinks. Also, I couldn't believe the bumper sticker on her car. "Proud parent of a Dr. Anderson patient."

That reminds me, this year I'm planning to make some elves for the front yard at Christmas. I know it's only February but it's never too early to plan if you want to draw big crowds.

Happy President's Month,
Randy Scuffle,
Case #2198

Dr. Anderson,

So it turns out those guys are building a fence around the yard. I pointed out that they forgot to put a gate in, but they just started talking in some other language and after about a minute I could barely imagine anymore what they were talking about. I tried learning a language once or twice but I always got distracted by the way it all made no sense to me. And when it makes no sense, the less I can concentrate on anything and I tune it out, like I do when the Bakers' dog starts barking every morning.

Except there is one thing I *can't* tune out and that has to do with my mom, whose TV keeps playing all night long. Between that and the guys building the fence and the dog barking I don't get any sleep at all. I was so tired the other day I accidentally kicked over one of my buckets and made a mess that won't come off the buggy. Also my shoes got pretty stained but the suit and the nose are okay. That was the first time in a long time since the big wood chip fiasco that I didn't get hurt too bad. Now I'm afraid something else might happen, since I escaped harm.

I did find a squirrel that almost drowned in my wiener soup bucket yesterday so maybe that's the bad thing that will happen. A bucket is more dangerous to a squirrel than to me. If I fell in the bucket I wouldn't drown unless my head weighed a lot more than my trunk.

Thank you,
Randy

P.S. Did you ever talk to your friend about my inner tube idea?

Dear Oscar Mayer™ Wiener Company,

I'm very disappointed that you apparently decided to support my son Randy's request for a lot of bologna and other meat products. He has been bragging around the dinner table that you have agreed to ship him all the meat he needs to develop the project he calls "across the fence." Randy doesn't need any meat. Especially wieners and bologna. He has enough of it. He even gets wieners from the Vienna Beef™ people, but they are people and not made of beef so don't get me wrong. He, as I told you before, eats it all constantly in his bedroom and sometimes even in the basement near the drain where I see remnants of wieners and other products. Some are chewed on and others look just shriveled up but they are all near the drain next to my laundry machines. It is quite often that I still do Randy's laundry since his accident with the turpentine. It really shouldn't have affected him the way it did, but he is really not himself anymore around solvents. My favorite way to do laundry (by the way) is late at night when it is still very quiet. I'm partial to fabric softener myself.

Twice now, I have been alarmed at Randy's requests for your meat, and I hope you really don't send it. I don't think you should as it will encourage behavior in my son that I don't believe there is a cure for, and that is: laziness! Also I don't want him to turn out stupid, which many magazines claim wieners will do if you eat too many of them. Have you done any studies on how many wieners or bologna products a person of Randy's age needs to eat to become stupid? Is it too late to stop? I think he is the type to smuggle bologna into the Betty Ford Clinic™ if he needs to undergo a process. If you have numbers of wieners that would help.

Also, maybe just so he doesn't get too alarmed when when you don't send his meat shipment, could you maybe give him a wiener whistle or a bologna poster? He would like that. He already subscribes to *Meat Processing* magazine. They don't have foldouts or anything but sometimes they have funny pictures on the cover.

Very sincerely,

Phyllis Scuffle (Randy the meat requester's mom)

Dear Electric Company,

I am enjoying a relatively hot summer in Chicago this year, and have heard that you will be providing your customers with rolling blackouts to save power and keep everything from blowing up the transformers again this year.

What I wanted to know was if anyone had ever suggested that customers organize rolling non-payment based on zip code. Like this month 60605 doesn't pay you or something? Please let me know about that. I would be happy to organize it if you want. Also, about how much electricity does it take to cook something without heat? Like how long would it take to cook my Thanksgiving bologna if I plugged it into the wall socket with a plug and some wires wrapped around it?

Do you have a cookbook for people like me who love to experiment with science and art? I really like to cook, but I don't have an ohmmeter or anything (not since 8th grade when I took electronics and that one kid plugged his project into the wrong socket and lost an eye.)

Thank you,

Randy Scuffle

Dear Mom,

Please do me a favor and get me some cooking oil the next time you go shopping. Also, the laundry machines and the TV in the middle of the night are keeping me awake when I could be sleeping or working on my art. I dream a lot of my ideas. I did write you a nice haiku when I was trying to get back to sleep. I hope you like it.

One more thing: when your friend Barry comes over the floor over my room creaks really bad and if I had to guess I'd say he was pretty fat.

Thanks for your respect of my dreams and wishes,

Randy (your son)

Dot on horizon
Endless wait for Clark Street bus;
Three of them arrive

Dear Emily,

I hope you remember me, because I remember you. You were the girl that I, Randy Scuffle, took to the prom in high school the year I had a date to go. You said I should call you or write to you when I had something more important in my life than my art but I want you to know that my art is more important to me than ever before. I say that if you go with me to the high school class reunion you will be among the most prized women there, as all the others will be looking at you because you will be with me.

See, I am working on a big project that will prove to be one of the most amazing art projects ever, and I am doing it for the reunion if it is approved as a plan. You should understand that if you decide to go with me to the reunion, you will also find out what it's like to be famous. I have all kinds of fame to my credit, but I am especially famous to an underground world of other artists and a few mimes. The reunion plan is bound to be fantastic. I will be showing some of my most detailed bologna people ever carved. You will want to shake hands with them and maybe even hug the one I plan to make that will look like Brad Pitt.

I once met a woman who used to be a personal cook for famous people. Her job was to make their food. Her job also included making sandwiches and so we had a very long talk about what kind of sandwiches they liked. She owns a restaurant now and all the reviews say it is good food so apparently if you make a sandwich for someone famous you can open a restaurant. At our reunion, you will see some very amazing things. I am going to start a whole new program of projects involving making statues out of meat but they resemble famous people. I want to pose them at malls and see how people react when they see Newt Gingrich or Justin Bieber but they are really made out of lifelike bologna. This is way better than wax statues or people painted like statues who scare you in European malls, as the bologna gently moves when you walk by or touch it. It would be nice if we could be friends again,

Randy Scuffle

Dear Dr. Anderson,

I know I haven't been coming in for a while now but I don't want you to think I'm never coming back. Everything has been pretty good now for about a month with the exception of my constant thoughts about elves. We talked about this before. I just keep asking myself questions over and over about elves and I wonder if that is one of the things that gives me problems. You said I could write you with any questions. I have lots of them. For one, I can't figure out why elves have to live in the woods. Or at the North Pole. Are there other places where they can thrive? Do they need extra water if you take them into the city or away from the woods or the North Pole? Maybe it's a sunshine thing and they don't like it.

Sunshine makes me mad when I get sand in my hair at the beach from a Frisbee that went by or that hit me in the ear. I got hit once in the back of the head with a roll of toilet paper at the Meatloaf reunion. Who brings a roll of toilet paper to a concert? While that is good food for thought, I mostly wonder about elves. I have all these questions and when I look online everyone just fights. Where do they shop? Especially now that the Wallaby Station™ at Diversey and Lincoln is long closed. Do they make all their clothes? Do they have a dress code? Do you *need* shoes in a forest where there are no people of normal size? I also wonder about this: what if elves have a normal-sized baby? Is it a giant? Or is it a normal size person? I can't decide yet if elves are the same species as people but from what I've seen in the drawings they appear to be happy. So they might be different. Do elves have their own mystic stories and do they follow the same astrological charts as humans?

The other thing that is really starting to bother me is the constant song about elves in my head. I constantly think it, and make up music for it but the words only go elf, elf, elf, elf, elf, elf, elf and sometimes in my head I believe I might start saying it on the bus. I don't want to be like the Thorndale Thorndale Thorndale guy. Would you be willing to ride my bus and see if the Thorndale Thorndale Thorndale guy is a future me? My mother says I don't need to take the bus but it's the only way to get where I'm always going. If you know of any elf books let me know. If you ever see one let me know too, I want to talk to him. That Will Ferrell movie about *Elf* answered none of my questions, and *Lord of the Rings* was too political.

Thanks Dr. Anderson, for listening to this letter,

Randy Scuffle (your patient)

P.S. What about fairies, dwarves, trolls, gnomes, leprechauns, munchkins, wallabies, smurfs, hobbits, gremlins? Are they related or different? I'll think about it and write later.

MAY 10th:

⊛ SAW GUY ON HALSTED Bus SAYING over + over:

"THORNDALE THORNDALE THORNDALE"

"ARISTOCRAT"

"THAT MAN HAS NO LEGS!"

⊛ ABOUT 20 TIMES

– get more buckets too
– polish shoes

Dr. Anderson,

I was watching the buckets of Sea Monkeys™ and thinking about how happy they must all be to know they live in a very predictable world and that they will soon be released to do the job for which they have been trained: eating brain plaque out of rich people's heads to keep them young. I'm sure they don't question each other about any of their motives and they don't need to hold meetings to try to agree what they want to do next. They already know. They know they will be soon munching out the destructive gunk that slows you down and makes you get wrinkly and forgetful. And that's about all they know. It's simple.

I'm not suggesting that this would be a good way for people to live, but you know, it made me think that one of the reasons it is so goofy in the U.S. now is because of one thing. Everyone is from somewhere else and they all bring new ideas about how to live. What makes it worse is that everyone is encouraged to be an individual and so then they even break out of whatever culture they came from. The advertisers are always telling us how important it is to be an individual and make the choice to drink Pepsi™ or drive a Dodge™. I always laugh a lot about how car companies say they is so different but I still count four wheels and a big gas tank as being pretty much the same. People don't get that even though they are individuals they really are all kind of the same.

Oh, I just remembered that I dreamed last night about a big tree frog that had jumped on my leg and I tried to get it off and it had really sticky pads on its fingers. It looked at me and said "I only want a free ride." So I put it back on my leg and took it with me. That was pretty normal for one of my dreams but it's the first time I've had a dream leave red spots on my leg.

P.S. My mom says we will be in soon for a visit. I don't know how we will get there though since the golf cart stopped holding a charge.

Randy

Dear American Express™

I am writing to you because you used to look for true stories about how the American Express™ card bailed people out of bad situations or allowed someone to have an exotic vacation despite some horrible tragedy. Besides, you have probably run out of stories about wayward Americans stuck in the middle of nowhere who were being abused by callous locals and then a call to American Express™ gets them rescued.

Too bad *Gilligan's Island* didn't have a phone; they could have called you and been rescued! They did have a phone in one episode but the operator thought they were kidding about being stranded on a desert island which, by the way, wasn't a desert island because of all the trees. Anyway, I want to share my story for your consideration.

As you probably are aware, I, Randy Scuffle, am quite well known for the unique art form I like to call "Good Neighbor Theatre." I was working on an idea I had and had once requested a grant from the people at Oscar Mayer™ and the Vienna Beef™ wiener companies. I was turned down for a grant on my project to study the psychological effect on rich young urban parents when they find meat in their yards. I am especially fascinated by the effect of wieners and bologna slices. Especially the effect these would have on the mother who got a lot of attention when she was pregnant but now faces the everyday realism of smelling ammonia and feces all day unlike in her prior career in advertising or marketing. Anyway, Oscar Mayer™ did not give me the grant. Neither did Vienna Beef™. I'm sure they would be happy to confirm that with you if you want. I have their addresses.

Anyway, thanks to American Express™, a card that's never turned down by the way, I put my art project funding on plastic. I was so pleased to receive my first load of bologna from the meat vendor. He accepted my card and turned over 31 packs of wieners and about 52 packs of bologna slices with no cheese bits (no pimento either: this is an American art project!) So I don't want to go into all the details now but I will give you some high points of my success on the project. The very first time I tried it, it was great to see a young mother examine a wiener that one of her daughters found in the sandbox! She wore a glove and poked at it. Then she made her daughter wash her hands. On another day, the father ran over a bologna slice with the lawn mover. He didn't notice when it shot out the side and hit the garage, but it drew flies nicely by the next day.

The project is far from over and I still have big plans! Thanks to American Express™ I will get a 50 or 70-pound giant bologna and carve it into a bologna child. This will be placed on our neighbor's porch during the night. The bologna child will be holding up a bowl and appear to be crying for food. But the bowl will be made of food, which is the "art." Thanks again American Express™!

Trustfully yours,

Randy Scuffle
Chicago, IL

> Found a parking space!
> But the meter is broken;
> Put a bag on it

Dr. Anderson,

I forgot to tell you about the guy who used to be president of this company I worked at, who used to just sort everyone's mail and look through the trash for pencil butts. Anyway, I accidentally spilled a bottle of corn syrup in the trunk of his car one time when he made me pick up his groceries. Then about a month later I had to drive the car to take his wife to the doctor with their kid, who was about 5 and still in diapers. The mom and dad thought he was a genius and that's why he didn't concentrate on toilet habits, probably because he was busy inventing a new creamed corn spoon for lazy babies.

So I'm driving their car, and I look in the back seat where he is sitting (in his own goo) and I see he is eating a bunch of ants off of his own arm like they are food. There were about a million ants in the trunk all feeding on the corn syrup. They crawled through the seat cushions and onto the kid, who probably had a bunch of them in his diaper when they got to the doctor's office. I hated having to drive them around. Last I heard the kid was accepted at some Montessori school because his dad donated a sandbox and inflatable helmets so the kids wouldn't get hurt standing in front of the swings all day.

I'm going to bed now.

My mom wants to know if I'm any better but she should probably ask you that directly.

Randy (your patient in Chicago)

Dear Grocery Store Executives,

Here is a test I made up for your stores to give to your potential grocery baggers. It's like a personality test but it is for the people who bag your groceries, so that makes it kind of moot, except at Trader Joe's, where they are pretty nice and don't mind my clown suit. The test begins here:

Before you can pack grocery bags, you must take this test. Don't start until we tell you to. Use a pencil. Don't take too long to think about it because you need to show you can pack a grocery bag in less than ten minutes.

1. Have you ever had to pay for your own food? (circle one)
Yes   No

2. What tastes better? (circle one)
- Bananas that look yellow and tasty
- Bananas that are bent in the middle
- Bananas that cost 80 cents a pound and you picked out each one personally because you have very particular needs but now that you get them home they are black smooshwads that leaked through the bottom of the bag because they were under a 5 gallon bottle of bleach.

3. If you spent $120 on food and got it home and it all looked like it had been sat on by a giant and the tomatoes were under cans and the bread was under a six pack would you rather:
- Just go back and beat the acorns out of the person who bagged your food
- Go back to the store and find the bagger's car in probably one of the prime parking spaces and smear a Cornish game hen all over the hood and windshield in protest
- Rub liverwurst into the bagger's hair

- Find out where the bagger lives and then one day go to their house and completely coat it with ground beef in the night

4. When you are packing people's food, do you plan to talk to the cashier about:
- Prices and other things related to the job you are doing right now
- Your car
- Your rotten miserable existence and how your parents and girlfriend hate you
- How the workers in the deli have a better union because they get longer lunches and an extra holiday off and when your next break starts

5. Which is heavier?
- Dry noodles
- A can of beans
- Taco shells
- Plums

6. What would you put on the bottom?
- Dry noodles
- A can of beans
- Taco shells
- Plums

7. Where is a safe place to put the plums?
- On top
- In a bag with other fruit
- In your pocket
- Between three two-liter bottles of Coke

8. What is the best place to put the ground beef?
- On top of the bread
- Under a six pack of beer bottles
- In a plastic bag on top of the canned goods
- In a separate bag with the ant bait and roach hotels

9. When is it safe to come over and meatball your house?
- Any time I pack the eggs vertically in the bag
- When I smell like bad cologne and have liverwurst in my hair
- I always wash my hands!
- When I accidentally dig my thumbnail into your tomatoes

> Fruit looks beautiful
> Waiting for it to ripen;
> Rots from the inside

Dr. Anderson,

I was watching an old episode of *Leave It to Beaver* the other day and made some notes I wanted to share. I know there are no *new* episodes but it made sense to me to point out that it was an *old* episode. Anyway, Theodore Cleaver, the youngest, is nicknamed "Beaver." In this episode, Clarence Rutherford, whose nickname is "Lumpy," was angry that Beaver called him "Lumpy." So he starts calling Beaver "Freckles" instead, causing a degree of anxiety in the Beaver that causes him to go home and try to scrape off his freckles with sandpaper. He also tries to cover them up with makeup, with unintentionally hilarious results. When he finally comes to terms with his freckles, he is again satisfied to be called "Beaver." It makes no sense.

In another episode, Beaver finds out that his teacher, Miss Landers, has a fiancee; this is a blow to Beaver since he has had a crush on her for years. The problem is made worse by the man she is about to marry (who incidentally wears is sweater around his neck and plays tennis, always a bad combination that spells danger in my book). He insists on calling Beaver "Teddy," which created anxiety in the Beaver once again. So this young child is traumatized by being called "Freckles." He is bedridden when called "Teddy." He wants, however, to be called "Beaver." That's no problem.

He wants to be called by the same name that we use to describe a member of the rodent family, which communicates by slapping its tail against the surface of the water. He makes no negative connection to the beaver's reputation for having unusually large and powerful teeth, or to its ability to cut trees with them. He is not threatened at all by the beaver's ability to coat itself with some kind of greasy funk that oozes out of its pores in order to provide a natural waterproofing while at the same time significantly increasing its buoyancy. Or that this animal has pockets of fat collected under its fur that are designed to keep it warm. Or that for many years beaver fur was considered suitable fashion. *None of this is a problem.*

Which is why I say Beaver Cleaver's family has a big job to do, fighting his natural inclination to become a feral beast, living in a closet or under the bed, gnawing spasmodically at furniture and leaving his stink in the carpet. I am so glad Miss Landers found a real man, or she would have to face the prospect of having this creature leer and hunt for her attention for years.

Thanks, Dr. Anderson, I had to get that out.

Randy

> Leave it to Beaver
> Why does he say he "thunked" it?
> I blame fat Larry

Dr. Anderson,

Last night I was just about asleep looking at the stars when I almost thought I was going to be taken by a spaceship. It turned out to be the Fuji™ blimp that was motoring around because I guess it was a night game at Wrigley Field. I forgot that without an overhead view of the field at night the game wouldn't look right on television. I don't know if the Fuji™ blimp is the one that takes the pictures or if it is the Metlife™ blimp, because I've seen that one too. It makes me kind of nervous when they are dragging their tails and fighting the wind because they look like they might fall out of the sky and they also look kind of obscene if you know what I mean. Anyway, it got me to thinking and I believe I have come up with a pretty good idea. I want to think about it more. Meanwhile, could you send twice as many rubber gloves as last time? I'm not always left-handed.

Thanks!

Randy Scuffle

Dear Oscar Mayer™ Wiener Company,

I have an idea that will help you out a lot, getting your name and products noticed in a good way. Remember your Wienermobiles? There used to be one parked near my house on Byron Street a lot in the summer, but it was faded and it didn't really look much like a wiener any more, at least it didn't have the same color as fresh wiener meat. It was more like the color of old plastic that used to be red and has been in the sun for a long time, like that big plastic salmon I once saw outside of a supper club on a trip through Wisconsin. Anyway, I couldn't figure out who would be leaving a perfectly good Wiener-mobile parked on Byron Street all the time but it must have been someone who had the keys.

Anyway, from my research I understand that there were never more than about 5 or 6 Wienermobiles in the world, and they were proba-bly made back in the era when Americans were being taken for a ride and cars were designed to last only 3 years instead of 4 like they are today, which means most of the Wienermobiles are probably not in really good shape anymore and should be taken off the road. Espe-cially if you have to mix gas with oil in order to make them go.

So here is my idea. Lots of other companies have blimps, like Goodyear™, and Fuji™ and Metlife™ and I think some others do too, but they never come to Chicago when I am looking up. You should make an Oscar Mayer™ blimp but have it be in the shape of a wiener or a Polish sausage or something long and made of meat. But not one of those cocktail franks because they are too small to fly. I've tried!

Here are the benefits: you could fly over Wrigley Field tempting people with wieners while at the game, thereby selling more wieners than ever before. It would look like a wiener, which would have no bad effects at all unless a really big seagull wants to eat something bet-ter than discarded french fries and hamburgers lying in a parking lot. Also, as far as whether the wiener blimp should look like a plain wie-ner or if it should be in a bun, putting it in a bun would only expose the tips of the wiener and kind of turns it more into a bun blimp that promotes the benefits of buns. You want maximum exposure for your wiener. You could then drop wiener whistles on the crowd at the game and if anyone gets one that is made of real meat they win a prize. Also, you *must* have your famous yellow and red band on the wiener to make it look really official. Wieners should not be seen without this band unless they are about to be eaten. It's like my mom always making me put on a towel after I run through the sprinkler in white shorts. Let me know if you need more ideas for this. I am willing to help out.

Randy Scuffle,
(Your number one wiener and bologna consumer in Chicago)

P.S. I like olive loaf too.

The most exciting family trip ever with my mom when we went to San Diego Comic-Con International and saw a wienermobile in the wild.

Dr. Anderson,

I decided not to wear the shoes. They got too floppy in the rain. So I'm going with the lumberjack boots. They are more waterproof and the pants tuck in pretty well. My mom brought me another bucket finally. She tried to trick me by the way with turkey wieners instead of beef ones. I know the difference because the soup made by the beef wieners is better and you can dunk bread in it. But only Wonder Bread™. It's the only kind I use if I haven't made shovel bread recently. Sometimes I wrap a soup wiener in Wonder Bread™ and eat it that way while dunking in the sauce. It's pretty good and you should serve it at one of your barbecues for your patients. They would like it and I'll be happy to tear the crusts off for you!

Mom wants me to wear more clothes but I told her the clown suit is great and breaks the wind just fine. If you talk to her tell her I'm warm from the fire. She won't believe me anymore. She always tries to get me to do everything her way and it drives me nuts. Like when I ordered some carving quality bologna for one project she thought she could substitute a coarse grind sausage and it didn't work as well. I tried it but it just didn't work. She says it saves money by not going with the top quality but I ask you, did great marble carvers of the Medieval days use chunky marble? No. They used the good stuff.

Back to my question. Did you ever say to my mom that I told you I had a dark spot in my mind? She says she knows about the dark spot and I say she doesn't. We argued about this until she went to sleep. I figured the rain would wake her up but the barking dog finally did it. After I made her take the turkey wieners back inside I saw one fly out the window hit the windshield of her car. It's one of those new bulgy cars like a blorpmobile and now she probably has a wiener streak on the window. That's how you know she's coming. Look for the wiener streak. By the way, she says she's coming to see you again.

Randy Scuffle

22

Dr. Anderson,

I've come to the conclusion that the wiener gun idea probably won't fly now since everyone has become so serious. I mean, it used to be that people would appreciate the art of it, but I don't think that is the case anymore. I suppose even if I did do that film project where I captured each wiener coming out of the gun in ultra slow motion someone would be offended because of that time I accidentally hit the pigeon with a cocktail frank. How could I know they had that kind of power? After that I had to be more careful and performed an experiment with a bologna statue I made for one of the presidential debates. I had this theory that the impact would either blow up the wiener or knock over Mitt Romney but it didn't. Instead the wiener just entered his leg and never came out the other side and the hole sealed up right away. When I tried to dig out the wiener from Mitt Romney's leg, I couldn't find it because it had become one with the leg.

Then some bird started boring holes all over him, despite his desire to become president. I thought at first it was a woodpecker but Mitt Romney was made of bologna like all my other debaters and it turned out that there were all kinds of worms that had made a million little paths and tunnels in his body because I forgot to do my soon-to-be patented Bolognafication™ process on the bottom of his feet. His presidential-like crust was okay but inside it was a mess. He still looked pretty good and you could never tell he was eaten up inside. Once all the beak holes were there the rain got in and the whole thing collapsed. So I donated that to the Art Institute but every time I go there I don't see it on display.

By the way, thanks again for the putty knife and the deer eyes. They look a lot better in the new Mitt Romney I am working on. The sheep eyes from that other supply house had a weird color. They were still better than the olives, but I did that just to figure out whether to make him look left or right. I'm not totally giving up the wiener gun idea. I've thought too much about it.

Bye,
Randy, your patient

Dr. Anderson,

So the police came to our house today and they were holding wieners. They say someone found the wieners in their yard and they have had reports that they are coming from around here. I can tell you right now these wieners were not from my wiener gun because I could see they didn't have the puffiness mine get around the base after they've been through the barrel. Besides, these were not even made of beef or pork or whatever they use to make wieners. You could see by their construction that these were clearly made of tofu, and I don't use tofu wieners for anything, not even for practice. That would be dumb. There is no way you can substitute tofu for wiener meat or even bologna because it just isn't the same. And the soon-to-be-patented Bolognafication™ process doesn't really work unless it is made of meat.

So my mom said they were wrong and made them go away, but the police said they would be coming back if there was more trouble. I think I can solve this whole misunderstanding but I've already used my allotment of bologna this week making that birdbath, which didn't really work out because I forgot that in the city there are a lot of carnivorous birds and they pretty much ate it instead of taking a bath in it. I even made sure the relief of Martha Stewart™ on the birdbath post was better than last time, when she looked kind of like a sole. All I had to do was reduce the size of her forehead and move one of the olives a little to the left.

So the first thing I need to do probably is get some more bologna. The weather has been cooler and the refrigerator isn't making all that noise anymore, so go ahead and send it. The last batch had a weird kind of skin on it that I had to cut through with a saw but that wasted too much and I used a wood plane instead. That worked pretty well, but I wasted a lot of time and when I got near the end of the project one of the ducks looked like it had a mousetrap jaw. I just couldn't get it right because the knife blade was too big and straight so I ended up having to bite the duck head into shape. It worked pretty well actually!

So now I have this idea that I want to honor future presidents by chewing his or her head out of bologna. I think that would mean a lot to whoever it is, knowing that I had to bite the meat into a reasonable resemblance. For once I'm glad I had braces. If you can start the paperwork for another grant I will start chewing some preliminary pieces, so they know it will be worth it. Also, would you please write to your friend, that Senator, and ask him if the President has thick or thin earlobes? You can't see that from any of the pictures.

My mom wants to talk to you about something, so she wants you to call. Right now I have to wrap the corn.

Randy Scuffle
(Chicago patient)

That pigeon is flat
Two-dimensional remnant;
Never saw the bus

Dr. Anderson,

Someone keeps turning off the electricity right when I am almost done grinding the nuts. The cord is plugged into the outside socket near the garage but I have an extension cord that has to run behind the fence along the alley and someone keeps pulling it apart. Did you know it takes almost 500 acorns to make a good sandwich? I also don't like it crunchy. I never understood why they started making it crunchy at the Skippy™ plant when it's easy to make it creamy. The crunchy kind always gets stuck in my teeth and sometimes makes the roof of my mouth hurt worse than Cap'n Crunch™.

But I can tell you this much about the squirrels in the neighborhood: they are almost impossible to catch without using some kind of bait. I tried three different formulas of what I like to call squirrel butter. Don't worry, it doesn't have any squirrel in it. I would like to market it in a squeezable container shaped like a big acorn but the top is soft and when you squeeze it a squirrel head kind of puffs out and the butter comes out of its mouth. But the problem with this is you have to use two hands to squeeze it and you end up with nothing to hold the pancakes down. Unless you use a stick or a shovel handle, but the shovel handle doesn't work when the pancakes are on the other end. And they're usually still really hot. I also have a recipe for shovel bread which is kind of good after you brush off the ashes. Anyway, can you see if a longer extension cord is available anywhere? I was going to go to the hardware store, but I'm having a reaction to something again.

Thanks!

Randy

Dear Randy,

As my patient, it is your responsibility to make and keep your appointments. Your mother says you have not been out of the yard for six weeks now. Why don't you come in at least once a week for a talk and then you can go back into the yard? You don't have to change your clothes or anything. Just come in. That will save your mother a lot of trouble. She is worried.

Thank you Randy,

Dr. Anderson

"You're on the love train!"
The Red Line was so much fun;
Robot conductors

Dear Dr. Anderson,

As you probably already know, the turkey wiener my mom threw at her car didn't bounce. It got stuck in the windshield wiper. Of course on her way to get me another bucket it started to rain and the wiener started to slurg and get turkey mung on her glass. When the police asked her about her license she blamed me! This is what I mean when I say she and I don't always get along. It's a good thing the wiener was cooked or it would have put an extra thick layer of grease on the window that only industrial cleaners or a Shawalla™ could get off. Now I know better than to let her into the camp. She was so mad and all she had to do was reach out and pull the wiener off the wiper and throw it away or at a bicycle or something, but instead she tried to drive by looking through the wiener smear. Now she is in the hospital again for some reason, and I never got my bucket. Can you send me one? I like red with extra thick plastic. I should get going now. The line at Hot Doug's™ starts getting really long and I want to get there before they run out of shrimp sausage.

Thank you, and I will try to come in this week.

Randy

Dr. Anderson,

I'm pretty disappointed about a project I was going to do but now has been usurped by the local government. They have gone and plastered the city with fiberglass cows all painted up weird and trendy. This is exactly what I feared would get in the way of my bologna people statues that were going to be seen around the city. Although cows make meat, these cows are fiberglass, so my people made of real meat would look like a copy of what they are doing with the cows. Unless of course I figure out a way to make all my bologna people into cowboys that are riding the cows and then I could make a statement about how if you eat cow you will become meat. It's like a transfer of the cow's soul if the soul is made of meat.

That would probably work too if all the cowboys were looking really bored. I think I could extend it and have some bologna bullfighters too and maybe some bologna rodeo clowns taunting the brightly painted cows with their weird costumes. This though would probably be a project best left for fall when it is cooler, despite my advances with the fly-repellent technique I apply to the bologna I select for sculpting. I'm afraid though that the cows will all be gone by then and the clowns will be taunting invisible cows. I should get going on this anyway. Also I think a good one would be to have a baby or small child stuck on one of the horns as if it were being gored by the cow. Bologna onlookers could then gasp in horror at the sight. I think flies would be a good touch on this one. I have to go now and thanks again for the markers and the soap.

Randy

Dr. Anderson,

Did I tell you about almost killing the crow with the wiener gun? Or did that email get lost too? I never kill anything but this was very close as I saw the feathers fall off the crow after it flew into the path of about a hundred wieners. I was trying to hit the Irving Park train platform; most of the wieners landed on the roof of the building next door, but one dropped low and first went though a tree where a crow was sitting and it flew off with feathers falling behind it. That one wiener must have been defective for it to drop like that. Unless it had a bent tip, but then how could it not jam in the gun like that time I loaded it up with those plumping hot dogs?

That was a mistake because once the barrel got all warm they jammed up really good. I had to let loose a bucket of Sea Monkeys™ to eat through the wiener meat in the barrel. It took about a month. Luckily I had a bad batch that acquired a taste for meat instead of brain plaque. Anyway, I'm thinking of how I can make tracer wieners that you can see in flight and help you aim like they do in the Army. Before you even say it, I already tried injecting some with ketchup, Jello™, and food coloring, which made everything I touched turn blue for about a week. I sure am glad I take my own showers now.

Bye,
Randy, your patient

Dr. Anderson,

This place I'm working looked at me kind of funny when I asked about the roof for my cubicle. All I want is something to shield the fluorescent lights and some of the noise from the giggling people in the kitchen. The soundproofing in the cube itself is probably better for hanging up pictures of dogs and cars than it is for soundproofing. Most of the sound bounces up out the cube anyway and everyone can hear every noise I make. Last time I was pretty happy and I think they liked the roof I built. The big benefit of corrugated metal is that you can actually have a second floor to your cube, and it helped make the lawn chair pretty stable. Plus you can fit more buckets up there; this cube only holds two buckets.

Everyone has been pretty nice here though. They all come by to look at what I've done with the artwork. Most of them are okay. Some of them are not, just like in the restaurant business, where a lot of customers probably have eaten a lot of server spit because they don't understand how restaurants really work. The other day I was at a place for lunch and there was a woman in there who made them cook her a special meal that wasn't even on the menu. The whole thing about "the customer is always right" is not a good thing from the employee's standpoint, and that applies too when you are working in almost any job.

Unfortunately for me a lot of times, my main customer is my boss. I can't figure out how if they are the customer, they can't seem to decide what services they really want to buy from me. They keep paying for it, but they never know what they really want. If you shopped for clothes the way companies shop for my services, you'd end up with a whole bunch of one-legged pants and bras that had no hooks and maybe belts with no holes punched in them.

By the way, I always thought a good art project would be to put Rogaine™ in someone's bra cups, although it would be most interesting if you just did the left one.

Randy

Dear Dunkin' Donuts™,

I was eating a donut the other day from Dunkin' Donuts™ and it was pretty good, just like always. Except for the time I got one that was raw in the middle it has always been okay! So while I was biting the donut it struck me that there was an opportunity for you to cash in on some other types of people who like meat more than custard. I know you've expanded your menu recently with ice cream and bagels, so it naturally follows that you are right on the cusp of meat. I could make a joke about bicuspids but that is obvious to you if you already know how to chew. Also you and I have canine teeth but we are not dogs. At least I am sure I am not a dog. I can bark when prompted though.

Anyway, you could get even more meat on the menu through the magic of filling donuts with ground chuck and you could still deep fry them with the current equipment all of your franchisees already lease. Imagine the beauty of getting a big mouthful of both your favorite donut flavor and the protein you need to make it through the day. You can cut down on the sugar rush that way by tempering it with meat. Ground chuck would be good. Naming the donuts would be fun and I would like to suggest a couple of things to you to get you started and I don't even want credit for it.

For starters I would call them "Beefnuts™" or "Chuckin' Donuts™." Or the best one yet: a "Holey Cow!™" If you added poultry to your menu they could be "Clucknuts™" or "Wattlesnax™." As long as you can guarantee people these would be beak-free these could become quite popular and I want to volunteer more ideas if you want them. Next time I eat a donut from Dunkin' Donuts™ I'm going to pretend it's filled with my favorite meat!

Thanks,

Randy Scuffle,
Chicago

Dr. Anderson,

I keep having these urges. Last night I stayed up almost all night imagining that I loaded up the car (the one that ran fine before my mom's wiener-induced accident) and started driving all over the country. Every time I would see a sign that said "Self Service" or "Self Parking" I would stop the car, get out with a bucket of paint, and cover up the "S" in "Self." At first I thought it would be a great holiday art project, like going around and rearranging all the neighbor's "NOEL" signs so they said "LEON." But then I remembered that elf dream I told you about and I'm wondering if maybe the elves are trying to tell me through my dreams that they are looking for a place to park their cars or to be served.

I remember in that dream, in which I worked with them for the longest year of my life making Christmas toys, that the elves had to have special cooling packs in order to come south of the Arctic Circle. The packs worked great until it started getting warmer. The area where they really started getting hot was a few degrees south of that, but it was close, and that's why they called it the "elf line." In case you don't know, it's between the Arctic Circle and the old Dew Line, which was a bunch of radar stations across Canada that warned us if Russia started lobbing bombs or space monkeys at us.

My mom said we used to have a bomb shelter, but she forgot where her dad put it. I should find it really. Especially now that it's this cold and I can hardly keep the wiener soup boiling long enough to keep the soup skin from coming back. Anyway, I bet if I find that bomb shelter there would still be some Cold War toilet paper down there.

Gotta go, Randy.

Dr. Anderson,

It has come to my attention that a bunch of my emails to you probably didn't get to you because I made a mistake and out of habit I typed .com at the end of your address instead of .edu. That means that some of my private stuff went to some company in Kansas City instead of you. I know that because I realized the mistake right after I sent it and then it didn't bounce back to me so I know it made it safely into their email nest, awaiting discovery. So if I made this mistake once I wonder how many times I've made the mistake, and do they have a whole bunch of my emails to you? I wondered why you didn't respond about the bendy pipe and Mason jar request.

Usually I have a new supply whenever I need it, but this time nothing ever came, so if you can, please send more bendy pipe and Mason jars. Also since the bendy pipe ran out I have also found a new use for glue, which I can explain later. Like my old boss once said, "It's completely intuitive once you understand it." My boss also said other things that I think I've told you about but I can't remember for sure and I don't want to repeat myself. Also, my mom is mobile again since she figured out how to remove the wheel chucks.

Randy

Dr. Anderson,

Today I feel like I'm all cooped up. Someone keeps looking through the knotholes in the fence again and I want to start throwing wieners at them or something but I'm afraid they might get the wrong idea and keep coming back to get more food. I just want them to go away. It's like when you keep getting asked to do something by your mom or some manager and they keep you really busy on a project. You finish it and then they say they want it done differently so you do it that way and then they change their mind again and you start to wonder if maybe they have worms or something. I don't think these are the kind of worms that eat you from the inside out but the kind of worms that get into your head and tell you that other people have somehow become your hands.

Everything you used to do with your own hands you have to make other people do. These are the worst kind of worms because they get into people and then they act like aliens who forgot how to feed themselves. Movie stars, some politicians, professional rich people and some people I have worked for are like this. I don't know how you catch these worms but I bet it's from sniffing something. I think the worm eggs jump off and get into your head and the next thing you know you're trying to protect your own hands from having to do any work.

I think if you could calculate the factor by which busy executives make other people do things for them you'd discover a whole industry of personal servitude but with better titles than "slave" or "assistant." It's either the worms at work, or it's just that there are many jerks in the world. I once had a dog named Mophead that I liked to make fetch stuff until one day he looked at me like he knew this would just keep going on and on. And ever since then I couldn't do it any more.

Randy

Dr. Anderson,

It appears that the money for an improved working version of the wiener gun will have to come from additional resources that I don't have right now, which leads me to wonder if I should get back in the stream of working again. I would only do it though because I think the wiener gun idea is a good one and I have made it work very well as it is but it has not evolved yet to be what I dreamed the other night.

I had this dream that I shot so many wieners at one of those big SUV cars that its windshield wipers couldn't keep up with the flow of splattering meat and the girl driving it had to take off her baseball cap and use the visor to scrape the wiener meat off of the windshield. The weird thing was when her dog started eating the wieners too, and I looked twice before I realized that the bandana she had put around its neck had a tag on it that said it was from Gap Dog™. This morning I got up and felt very strongly that another way I could do a short art project in the meantime would be to put a wiener under the windshield wiper of every SUV in our neighborhood. I could do this early before they come to ticket your car for not moving for street cleaning.

I bet the cars that got tickets would look funny if the Chicago police attached the ticket to the wiener. Birds could pick at them too, so it is organic art, and in a way, the project would be distributed a lot further than just in the neighborhood. Anyway, I might have to get a job because the wiener gun still needs perfecting. I need more air pressure and a better way to keep them from bending as they come out of the barrel. Only a few of them really get to the el-stop from here. If you can think of any way to help fund the wiener gun project so I don't have to get a job again then let me know because I'm afraid I'll have to work with people who like sports. It's bad enough that some guy in our neighborhood always opens his door and yells "da bears" every time his team scores a point. It is annoying but frightening too since he is a grown up and has children. And drives a car. If it had an old-style long antenna I would put a wiener on it.

Randy
Your patient.

Dr. Anderson,

I'm feeling pretty good today, especially now that the gophers have given up. Sometimes you can't tell whether they're just going to hide out for a while or whether they are just going to fight you until you have to take drastic measures. I hate having to do that since I really like nature. These gophers dug all under the yard and porch and I'm pretty sure they chewed through some of the cable TV stuff I had out here. The gopher wars were good for me to keep me occupied with something other than wanting to throw potatoes at my mom. Ever since she got back from the hospital things have been really weird.

The other day this truck pulls up with a bunch of guys in it and they deliver a big box and ever since then all I hear is my mom playing a new organ upstairs in her room. It's one of those really big ones with three keyboards and a whole lot of pedals which she can barely reach even when wearing those rubber buckle boots that she keeps calling slippers. I told her about 11 times that they were boots, not slippers, and she just keeps saying that "for slippers, they have really good grip."

All night long she plays songs that don't belong on the organ. Some songs are made for the organ but not the Rolling Stones and the Sex Pistols. Where do you get sheet music for that? And I also can't tell if she's slowing it down on purpose or if that's the way she hears it in her head. Maybe I'm wrong though. My timing has been off ever since the accident with the clam chowder. That was a bad weekend.

Randy (your patient)

Dr. Anderson,

Would you please print this out and mail it to my mom? She won't come out even when I ask her nicely through the amplifier. Thank you.

Mom,

I need a couple of things since the fence went up. More food is one thing and I also need four hundred or more eyes from that taxidermy catalog laying on my dresser in the bedroom. Please order the ones that look like DEER eyes and not the GOAT eyes, as the goat eyes have horizontal slits that look terrible on the beef babies I am making for my next project called "Bologna Ward™."

Thank you!

Randy, your son.

P.S. I dare you to play "Free Bird."

Dr. Anderson,

You asked once in a previous meeting if I could think of anyone I admired or liked as if it were a hero of mine. I have thought a lot about this in between my projects or even while working on my projects. Especially the current project that involves me hiding out as "the camping clown." While I wouldn't exactly say that living in the backyard of my mother's house is hard camping, there are wild animals that come through here like cats, crows, squirrels, a guy looking through all the garbage cans and a ton of worms since it's been raining so much lately.

The worms look a lot like living wieners, but right now I'm pretty set since before my mom went into the hospital after the wiener induced accident she did some shopping and got me plenty of meat. I have been thinking a lot about this lately and it seems that if wieners were alive you wouldn't be able to tell which end is the head. Also it is pretty hard to tell the boys from the girls. I'm going to research this more and let you know my findings. Since I'm in contact with a lot of wieners lately I figure I'm pretty much in a good position to do the testing.

Anyway, back to the question you asked me about who I admire. I have to answer right now that I think the man I most admire and would consider my hero has to be Geppetto, since he is the one who figured out how to bring wood back to life.

I'll get back to you on the tests,

Randy

Dear Dr. Anderson,

I think I have to rethink my idea about using hard boiled eggs for eyes since as soon as you carve out enough of the white so you can see the yellow, the yellow pops out from the pressure of the shrinking meat-head sculpture. I was letting the first version of Bob Saget cure in the corner where a big puffball was growing and I looked over in time to see his eyes blow out and fall on the ground. Unfortunately, it didn't make the sculpture more accidentally artistic like when they make a really bad movie but a core of people think the director is making some deep satirical statement and the movie ends up being popular or respected. I think you could say that happened with *Gilligan's Island.*

The *Brady Bunch* is that way too, where the point they are always trying to make is that Jan is tired of not having privacy but the directors and writers by accident point out that the family uses her as a kind of slag heap for all of their anger and disrespect. I always felt sorry for Jan because she ended up more than once begging to be treated like dirt if only the family would accept her again. So the Bradys were pretty mean to Jan, and even though she wasn't a pigeon-toed redhead, I kind of liked her. Cindy was just a head on a stick. Peter was a cloud of nothingness. Marcia was a snotty little creep and Greg's shoulders needed to be put back on another monster body. And if my little brother had been Bobby I would have turned him into bologna art. But I wouldn't even use olive loaf, which I consider to be my Italian marble; I would have used that cracked pepper stuff that no one buys. Anyway, I will try to make Bob Saget look more surprised without the use of eggs in his head.

Randy

Dear Hot Pockets™ People,

Your product Hot Pockets™ that you sell by saying "when you're hungry for a meal that's not a big deal, what are you gonna have? Hot Pockets™!" drives me nuts. First, the people look way too happy, like their lives revolve around these microwave snacks that probably feeds about one person who isn't very hungry but you show a whole family being fed and still having the energy to grow and laugh out loud. Plus they all have perfect teeth which I don't think many people who eat like that have.

But back to the second reason and maybe the most important reason why your product drives me nuts: *hot* rhymes with *snot*. So in my mind when I don't have the elf song going, I keep thinking you're singing about "Snot Pockets." Not only that but you're trying to get me and my mom to eat them and grow and laugh out loud. My mother never laughs much anymore, not since January when she got that letter. So when you tested the product song did no one point out that it rhymes with snot? If they did, were they made hungry by that? Is there a hidden appeal to eating snot? I remember Brian Addison in third grade was a booger eater and he didn't know we watched him eat boogers all day. He ate them for breakfast. I saw him eat some at lunch period, and I know for sure he ate them at home because even his sister said he was a gomer and a troll.

I hope I am wrong about this but what if you really are selling snot pockets? Who makes them? Do you hire a bunch of sick people to blow their noses in dough pockets before flash freezing them for freshness? Or maybe children would work better. They don't have to be sick and they always have runny noses. You could get in trouble with the law if you sold sick snot instead of healthy young snot. Snot should be fresh and not filled with any bacteria that could sicken your customers who would then sue you. Does the microwave action at cooking time dry out the snot pockets? How do you keep that from happening?

Thank you for your fresh products,

Randy Scuffle

Dr. Anderson,

I was on the train last night (car 3666), and there was this guy with his two kids and they were climbing all over the seats and the guy was telling them to hang on tight. He was doing that because the train wasn't riding very smoothly. It was jerking around corners a lot like it was being pulled by a team of one-legged turkeys. He didn't make them sit down or anything either. The weird thing was that you could tell that a lot of the people who were standing were starting to wonder if they had to catch the kid if it fell because the dad obviously wasn't going to do anything about it. I know I was, and that's were my moral question comes in.

What if I was a guy with a hook for a hand? Would I be morally obligated to try to catch the kid, even if they ended up stuck on my hook? Or would I be morally obligated to protect the kid from the meathook effect and hope they bounce off of something else instead? I'm thinking that I should have prepared better. I bet you could protect a lot of children with a wine cork on the tip of the hook. Not one of those fake corks either, it would have to be a real Portuguese cork. I could then catch the kid if it fell and the dad wouldn't want to sue me.

The other thing that might work though is a quick-release hook that would allow you to shake off anything that got stuck on it, but that doesn't solve the moral dilemma. When a group of people got off the train at Fullerton, one of them said to the dad that watching his kids had convinced him not to have children. Anyway, I'm glad I don't have a hook, but I wonder where these things come from.

Randy,
Your patient on the north side

Police Blotter, Lakeview: A report of a body found at the Karl Siewers Playlot on Grace street turned out to be, in reality, a human form that had been carved out of a large block of unidentified meat product. Police say they received a call Thursday at 8:12 pm saying that the body of a child had been found wrapped in a blanket. According to the coroner at the scene, the carving was "quite lifelike," and had the proper density and weight to appear to be a real body. It is another in a series of events in the Lakeview area that have neighborhood watch groups alarmed. In July, another apparent body was found in the back yard of a residence on North Greenview street.

"It's really disgusting," says Wendy Zimmerman, secretary of a local neighborhood group. "I don't know why this is happening. The neighborhood really is on the way up. Something like this can affect our property values." Police say there is really nothing illegal about the activities, unless they can cite the perpetrator for illegal dumping. "Mostly, it's just very frightening to whomever finds the 'bodies,'" says police district supervisor Aaron Gardling. Zimmerman adds that the neighborhood is important for the children. "We want an atmosphere here that will demonstrate that our decision to petition for zoned parking was a good one. How can we justify this as a special neighborhood when people find ham-babies on their back porch every morning?"

Another, earlier, series of vandalism this summer has not yet been linked to the meat bodies. In those incidents, slices of what appeared to be bologna had been hung from trees using Christmas tree ornament hooks. Police are asking anyone with any information to call district headquarters.

Dr. Anderson,

What are the chances I could get another shipment of cotton balls? I discovered a problem with the Sea Monkey™ nests after it was too late. Now I have to start over again with new ones. The training though is going well and I think I found a group of smart ones. The best part of it is that they seem to have a voracious appetite for wiener. Even better than the squirrels have in spring. There was one squirrel last year that figured out how to climb into the bathroom window and it ate a hole in the side of the Brad Pitt head that I carved for my mom's birthday. It ate through the one spot I didn't glaze all the way and then it made a nest inside and had babies. My mom didn't even know it because she had all her dolls piled up around the Brad Pitt head.

One doll that I think was designed by Marie Osmond got a bunch of wiener chips all over it from the squirrels chewing action. At first my mom thought the Marie Osmond Doll™ had chewed through the Brad Pitt wiener head because it came with big smiling teeth that could have been pretty sharp. I told her it couldn't have been the doll because its bite marks didn't match what was on the wiener head and she calmed down.

The hard part was getting the baby squirrels out of the head and I didn't want to keep hitting it with a stick or it would crack. I used the head to hold up her bathroom window but faced the hole to the outside so the squirrels thought it was a tree or something and when they got old enough, they left home. Now we have a cork in the side of Brad Pitt's head, which is okay because it keeps the smell out of the house.

I just dropped the shovel bread on the ground, so I have to go now.

Randy

Doctor Anderson,

I agreed to write to you more frequently about how things are with me since starting with the art projects as a way of distracting my mind from the thoughts that distract me. So far everything is pretty good but I still have thoughts about my former boss at that company I told you about so many times in those meetings we used to have. I find myself in bed at night and even sometimes during the day thinking about how to let him know how much I hated working with him after he revealed his severely disturbed qualities.

So the thing I am thinking about lately is how to meatball his house. I plan it all the time. I think about what kind of meat to use, and have settled on ground beef but with a high fat content that will probably draw more flies than real lean stuff. I only know that most people are attracted to fatty foods so probably the flies will be that way too. Plus it would be cheaper to do it with high fat content ground beef and then I could do a more complete meatballing episode. I have decided that the best thing to do would be at night and it should be during the summer so that the maximum slime and fly activity occurs. I don't know if I should do one full pound or two. I figure the meatballs should already be made and I should probably wear gloves. It would draw less attention to the meatballing if I rode a quiet bicycle to the scene of the event because I could make a faster getaway. I could throw the meatballs at his house, maybe hit the door a few times, and then take off.

My real big dilemma though is if I ditch the gloves at the scene, could they make molds of the gloves with some kind of spy clay and reproduce my hands and arms and then somehow identify me as the meatballer? But if I don't ditch the gloves right away, like maybe a block later, then my handlebars will get full of meat and they will attract flies. This could be bad when trying to avoid the police because they could just look for a bike with lots of flies and a guy swatting all over while riding down the road. I guess another potential problem would be if on the way there the meatballs somehow fell through the basket and onto my wheels which could be a problem in two ways: first, I could slip and lose control on the meaty wheels; second, and most concerning to me, is that I'd have ground beef flung all over the back of my clown pants. That would be hard to explain if the police saw all the flies. So the reason I'm writing to you is this: Is it wrong to meatball someone's house if you call it an art project?

Thank you for reading,

Randy Scuffle
P.S. I think I should come in soon for a check up.

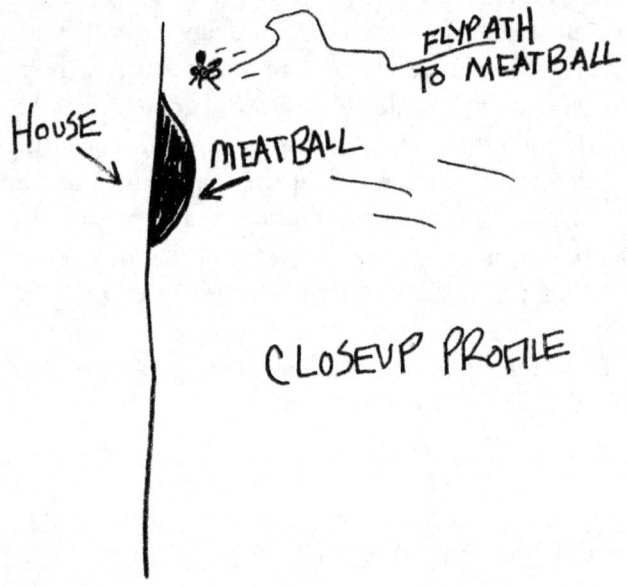

Dr. Anderson,

I remember once when I was a kid there was a poster of a guy in a car offering kids a bag of candy to get in the car with him. That was right around the same time when the most dangerous thing you could do was pick up a blasting cap. There used to be a lot of warnings about blasting caps but now you never hear about them anymore. Did they stop making blasting caps or did they just get better at not leaving them laying around for kids to play with? Now you see posters for needles and drugs and all kinds of interesting things. All we had was blasting caps. I never found one but I was always looking for one so we could use it to blow up something like a can filled with mud or even some kid's bike. I think I told you about the burning tennis ball, which was very interesting and left a slime trail on the street for a long time. I stopped playing with explosives though after having to wear a wig for the big recital.

Randy

Don't step in the puke!
Hey you, take off your headphones!
You just stepped in puke!

Dr. Anderson,

I can't say how much effort it took for me to keep from speaking my mind to a woman on the train the other day when I saw she was trying to clean up her face after sneezing by using this very nice handkerchief. She was a very elegant woman kind of trying to clean herself after a facial snort and I know she was doing a good job of following all the procedures as outlined in the little etiquette book we all have in our heads. So the main reason I felt really weird about this whole dainty exhibition was that I realized just how easy it would be for her to stuff the whole handkerchief into one of her massive noseholes. They were huge. Both of them. She could have accidentally just jammed one up there with a quick thumb poke and it would be gone.

But this also reminded me of the need, again, for nosehole tampons. I know I have probably told you about this before, but I think they are a good idea and much needed. What about if the nose tampons were prepared by dipping them in something that would repel blackheads from the inside? I can't figure out yet whether it would be better to have them attract or repel them. If you sucked the blackheads into the inner sanctum then you would never see them, but if you pushed them out of a nose you would encounter potentially embarrassing problems at cocktail parties or during SAT testing. Anyhow, I just thought you might be still interested in this idea of tampons for noses. They would be big sellers during cold and flu season, and once it became socially acceptable to wear them, think of all the extra work you could get done by not having to take your hands off the keyboard to blow your nose all day. Also I have some ideas for names and I think I need to keep working on it since the best one so far is Booger Corks™.

Bye,
Randy

Dearest Dr. Anderson,

My son Randy, a patient you've been treating for bologna diseases, insists that there is nothing wrong with going out at night wearing that stupid clown suit. I fear for his life! Is there some trick I can play on him to change his mind? Or what? By the way I can't begin to thank you for the wonderful new organ. I love it! I've been learning to play some wonderful music and I've turned my bedroom into a recording studio. Can you send more egg cartons? My friend Iris says they absorb sound so the paint won't chip so bad, but I ate so many eggs last week that Randy's bologna bucket soup is starting to look good (which I'm sure has no vitamins in it at all, not after all that boiling.)

Sincerely,
Phyllis Scuffle

P.S. Thank you also for the bumper sticker! It's been on the car since you sent it and I hope you get some business from it.

> ## Proud Parent of a Dr. Anderson Patient

Dr. Anderson,

I couldn't help but be alarmed recently when I noticed that the people park on Sheffield just south of Diversey has been turned into a dog park and now people can't get in. They cut out all the grass and trees and then they paved it with asphalt which if you ask me is less like a dog habitat and more like a person habitat. People usually do that for themselves, not for other animals. I don't get it. So now if you want to go to that park you have to be a dog, and there are lots of them there too!

But the goofy thing is that in addition to all the dogs there are people just standing around talking about dogs. If I put on a dog head and ran around in the park would they take me to the pound if no person claimed to own me? Can homeless dogs use the park I guess is what I'm asking? There is a fence all around it and there are gates; I don't know of any dogs with hands or thumbs, so for the most part they can't get into the park if they are homeless. I think this is discrimination against the homeless dogs. By the way, there used to be homeless people sleeping in the park but they seem to be gone now too because the only place to sleep is on turd-coated asphalt. Although I did notice that they have also painted the asphalt green to further approximate what a dog would perceive as grass if it could only see in color.

By the way, I am through with the bucket project now. I just got a new Rubbermaid™ catalog under the fence and it has some pretty neat stuff in it for future projects like the one I'm still formulating. If you need any kind of container let me know and maybe we can order some and get a discount. I will for sure be ordering something to keep all the leaves in.

Randy

Dear Dr. Anderson,

Please pass this along to your friend at Public Television WTTW when you see him next and tell him he should read it. (In a nice way.)

Dear WTTW,

I can't take it any more. I have to let you know about how much you are just making me really mad. Out of the more than 73 channels I have on cable, how many television stations actually ask for money? One. Yours. It's the only one. How many have commercials? All of them. Even yours. Can't you figure out how much to charge them or something? Everyone else can (even Animal Planet™) and they're not even listed in our cable guide.

But you claim your station is different because you say you have all these different shows on that you can't get anywhere else. Yet you used to show the 1996 ballroom dancing competition or maybe the 1988 or 1989 competition, but they all look the same. The dancers are all too tan and tight and stretched out. And the announcer keeps saying that the partners are 'capable.' That's what they say at the dog shows too, only they say it about the owner or whoever it is that runs around and tries not to slip in something left behind, which probably embarrasses the dog and then the judge has some kind of markdown for when your knee has grass stains on it.

And then in between segments of the show, people who wear ugly sweaters come on and try to tell me that they actually watched *Monty Python* when they were growing up. Then you laugh as I pledge and never again see *Monty Python*. In short, if you want us to believe that we can't see programming like yours anywhere else, add some variety to your schedule, and make sure no other cable station is showing the same stuff. On the other hand, you could let loose a million gophers in the USA. Then *I* could laugh at *you*.

Thanks for being open minded,

Randy Scuffle,
Citizen

Dr. Anderson,

Thanks again for the plywood. It's helping a lot with the wind if you keep away from the knotholes. The sound level has dropped off considerably, and I have had good results with the initial experiments. Here is an idea that we could probably make some money off of and you wouldn't have to do the work. I would be happy to do all of the work if you would just use some of your contacts in Hollywood to help get this going. When I worked at the radio station that one summer I played with a lot of the sound effect records they had and I noticed something really strange. They never had any of the sound effects I wanted to hear. I already knew what a motorcycle sounded like and I knew what wind and hail and creaky doors and cats and walking sounded like. That's all they had on those records, which was kind of disappointing when you need to know what it sounds like when ham is dropped on stainless steel. And what kind of a business is that anyway to just have sounds we already know?

So what I want to do is record all the things that no one has ever heard before, like what does it sound like when you kick a cocktail frank into a Twister™ mat hanging from a clothesline? Or, what does it sound like when you drop an apple pie on the floor? I always wondered if it was different when it was hot or cold due to the spreading factor of hot apples. I think it would be different because the hot one would probably have less of a flump sound and more of a plock because of the spreading.

We could sell the sounds to the movies and if ever any of these sounds were needed they wouldn't have to wonder what they sound like or make them up. Like they used to do with thunder. Instead of recording real thunder they used to bang on a sheet of metal. People know it's not thunder. Too many of the sounds now in movies are cartoony versions of very normal things. That doesn't work right.

Here are some other sounds I want to record, which I can do here in the plywood hut until winter gets really cold. But then I can record winter sounds anyway so it just might continue to work, like what a frozen wiener sounds like when you hit it with a big hammer on many different kinds of wood. I am sure mahogany would sound different than koa or pine. And another thing, I bet the frozen wiener brand makes a difference too, especially if it is one that has been pre-filled with cheese. I have to go now. Anyway, think about it and if you want to do this, let my mom know because when I told her about this, she thought it would be a good idea for me to get some exercise.

Bye,

Randy

> Don't touch the third rail
> Never pee on the third rail
> Welcome to heaven

Dr. Anderson,

I am completely frustrated by the inability of the United States Postal Service™ to send you those pictures of corn-animals I made. They keep sending it back to me saying your forwarding order has expired, yet the yellow sticker on the envelope clearly says your new address. So they can deliver it far enough to put a sticker on it with the new address and then they deliver it back to me, wasting twice the time and money. It's no wonder they are falling apart.

I do my best to recycle the junk mail, which I usually use to make my own paper, using window screens and flat pieces of wood to squeeze the juice out.

I tried once to make Sea Monkey™ paper but it didn't hold up very well when you tried to write on it. After all the mashing I did I figured it would work better, but it also attracted cats. I made a bologna dog to scare them away but cats have another sense or something that allows them to know there are no bones in bologna dogs, and they walk right past them. My mom says cats can smell your marrow, and that's why she never let me sleep with the window open. I don't know why they would only smell your marrow when there are other things to smell like earwax. But I suppose you have to leave something for the birds to pick at if you die. My mom said I would die at night if I didn't pray not to die, so I prayed that the cats couldn't smell my marrow. Then when I found out about birds, I had to pray twice as long. Nothing killed me in my sleep the one time I forgot to pray so I figure it's more luck than anything else.

Did you ever wake up in the middle of the night and think your pillow was filled with blood, but it turned out to be a shadow in the indentation where your head was? I did.

Randy

Dr. Anderson,

Thank you for agreeing that it is okay for me to continue writing you the answers to the questions you send me. It's probably best that I don't come in anymore for a while, especially since the accident with the french fries. Tell your receptionist that I am sorry and I didn't mean anything by it.

I've had a lot of time to think about stuff since my mom has been in the hospital again, this time for those half-pound bunions she had removed, and I started getting really nervous about when she might come home and what if I have to start changing her diapers or something all of a sudden. But she called me yesterday and said I had to take the foil off the canopy I put over the card table in the yard. So I know she is still okay.

Someone in the neighborhood is telling her stuff too, and I can't figure out who it is. One thing I really want to tell you about is that I discovered something about a week ago that is revolutionary. I was thinking hard about some stuff and getting ready to write to you when I realized that my thoughts had become clear. When I wondered why that must have happened so suddenly I realized I had been holding a potato in my hand the whole time. It's weird that I think there is the calming influence of a potato.

I wonder how far that could go. I bet dentists and proctologists would welcome the concept. They could make their patients hold onto a potato while they are being worked on. That's a lot cheaper than drugs and I bet you could sell a lot of premium special potatoes to the New Age people who are always looking for some crystal or something. Doctors who believe in the calming influence of potatoes could have the international symbol for potatoes on their white coats.

Potatoes rot though. And what do you do when the potatoes are sick? No wonder the Irish were really on edge during that famine. Probably I'll have to investigate the possibility of putting the potatoes through the soon-to-be-patented Bolognafication™ process; it seems to work because the neighbors don't even complain anymore about the buzzing sound.

Randy Scuffle (your patient in Chicago)

Dr. Anderson,

Remember that time I wrote about the songs in my head and was having a hard time deciding if I was crazy or creative? I wrote out my feelings about the music that never forms into regular bars or graphs and goes around like Brian Eno on a tricycle. It worries me sometimes. I can't write music, but it is always there. Like a theme. I also wanted to let you know I'm ready to talk about that dream I had about Bea Arthur.

In it, I saw Bea as a spokesperson for a new product, a kind of gum that is pink and tastes like shrimp. She would look me right in the eyes and say "Shrimp gum, Walter?" I am aware that most advertisers use sex to sell their products, so you might wonder as I did why I still wanted to actually try the gum in my dream. I still to this day wonder how good shrimp gum must taste. How can that be, and what does it mean that Bea Arthur represents some kind of trustworthy figure that could offer me something pink and chewy that I'd want to put in my mouth? And I think about this a lot!

The idea though would be pretty good for a company that wanted to get away from the regular mint and cinnamon flavor gum that every gum company makes. If gum could be made in regular food flavors then maybe people wouldn't want to eat so much and if the gum tasted like their favorite Hungry Man™ dinner dessert or even like meat you could really get people excited. I would still put in some caffeine though because you really do need something to get them hooked. I think meat flavors of gum would help so many people. I also would make sure that it didn't give you beef or pork breath but instead had some kind of chemical like chlorophyll in it so that it would mix with your spit and not offend everyone at work. I'm sure people out on kissing dates would appreciate that too!

Here's another twist to the story. Let's say you and I invest in this company of gum. I would suggest in our product planning session that we make the gum shaped like the food that it tastes like. An example would be a little steak for beef-gum and a shrimp for the shrimp-gum. But then we could argue at length about whether or not the theme is correct when a shrimp is a shrimp and a steak is just a part of a cow. Would we just do shrimp parts like shrimp hips?

Would anyone know what that was? The other way is to argue that we make everything whole. Like a little cow shaped gum for beef-gum and a little piglet for pork-gum. The pork-gum would be kind of pink too unless we got some food coloring and made it look like it had been in the mud. But that could be another business with chocolate piglets! I'm getting very excited about this and wonder if I need your help more for the business or for the ideas that get in my head. Let me know soon, so we can meet. Also, if we made subgum flavored gum it would be subgum gum.

Randy Scuffle
Chicago

HI! I'M A SHRIMP!
I'M MADE OF GUM!
UNLIKE MY FRIENDS AT
RED LOBSTER, YOU CAN CHEW ME
FOR HOURS! AND I WEAR A HAT!
AND I STILL HAVE A FACE!

Dr. Anderson,

I was thinking yesterday on the train (car 3336 again!) about what would happen if you were standing on the edge of an elevator shaft with someone you didn't like very much and just because you didn't think very much about it you pushed them into the elevator shaft. But in my mind everything always goes wrong even when I am getting revenge for something.

This time, I imagined that it would be just my luck that when I pushed this person into the elevator shaft they would grab at my brown sweater and pull me in with them. On the way down I figure I would be pretty sorry I did this and I'd have about a second or two to realize that this was it. I'm pretty sure I would be dead in this episode since the fall would be dramatic from about the 40th floor. So then I wondered if we both died and there is such a thing as souls, how would they get out of the elevator shaft? Would they be stuck or could they go through walls and go wherever souls go when they are freed from their slavery of having to live in warm meat? And then it started to bother me a lot that if they couldn't get out very easily they would be mixed around together with all the air pumping in the shaft once they got it working again after washing out the bottom.

What would happen if the souls showed up wherever they go after death and one now had 30 percent evil in it and the other one had 30 percent less evil in it? How would they count that? An evil person shouldn't get elevator shaft credit and not have to go to hell or wherever if they were 100 percent evil before the episode. And a good person that was 100 percent good shouldn't become part evil and have to go to purgatory or wherever if they should go straight to heaven if there is a place like that.

Randy

Dear. Dr. Anderson,

I hope you can see my son Randy soon. He has been acting a little out of bounds lately and I don't know if it's something he can solve by himself or if the problem is mine. Yesterday he wouldn't even swallow his meat loaf. He just kept chewing and chewing and chewing. It was disgusting. The whole time he kept writing in a book and spitting in a cup which then of course I had to wash. I wanted tongs for hands after watching him eat! This is not normal for Randy as he usually eats pretty well, especially meat loaf. His other doctors say they are sure he will grow out of it but they were saying that years ago, too! I'm pretty concerned. I don't know how he can get any calories just from chewing. Is it possible? Also don't worry about insurance or payments or anything. We have money left over from some of the accidents.

Thank you for treating my son!

Phyllis Scuffle

Telescopes are blind
The urban night sky hides this:
History of stars

Dear Sprocket Company,

I have used your sprockets for years and have always found them most satisfactory, especially for clever non-industrial applications for which I have won several awards from governments, universities and the recently-discovered secretive for-profit branch of public television. Until recently, your sprockets have always arrived wrapped in heavy paper so that the lubricant didn't get absorbed by the shipping box. Now you have chosen to deliver them in those goofy foam noodles, which do nothing but wick away the oil and it migrates to the edges of the box where it soaks through.

By the time the mail person delivers it they think my mom has sent me a very heavy cake that you probably couldn't digest if you wanted to. It's like when you turn 25 and discover that fast food hamburgers aren't really processed by your body the way other food is. For one thing my mom doesn't make cakes and when she did in the past they weren't that heavy unless it was my birthday special cake with all the ham in it.

So now when I come home and see this greasy box on the porch I know your sprockets have arrived. However, I am torn between happiness and dread because now I have to spend about two days picking off the little goofy noodle bits that have clung to the sprockets in all the tiny spaces. I must inform you that these goofy bits are not good for the type of things I invent and the only place to wipe them is on my pants. The winter weight clown pants with the potato pockets are the best but that won't work in the summer; besides, why waste good clown pants on sprocket goo?

My mom said a long time ago that the only time you wipe anything on your pants is when everything else around you is too smooth. Please change your ways and decide to wrap your sprockets in paper again.

Randy Scuffle

Dr. Anderson,

It was so cold this winter that the squirrels now love to eat wieners. Lately they've been coming around more and more. They will eat out of my hand whether I'm wearing the gloves or not. If I hold a wiener in each hand there will be at least five or six squirrels on the card table eating at them. They have a look in their eyes that shows how much they trust anyone with good food and, as a side benefit, they appear to not be affected by the big red nose.

I wonder if people would take food from anyone no matter what they looked like or would they have to take it from someone who is only beautiful? For example I wonder if people would take food if their waiter was a hunchback? What if the cook was a hunchback? What if the servers were all really beautiful and attractive people and it was a famous restaurant but the chef was a gargoyle-faced hunchback that had to be wheeled around on a cart because he had no legs? The "torso chef" he would be known as, probably. Would people still eat what he cooked even though he was considered ugly by many people and all the food was really good? I am developing a theory on this. I'm pretty sure that if the chef is ugly it would be considered part of the food-art; but if the waiters were all ugly no one would eat there no matter how beautiful the chef is.

This also makes you wonder about the whole famous chefs thing. People rave about certain chefs, and really all they do is prepare what you are going to digest. Mostly, all food looks the same in the end. It can cost $3.99 or $75 a plate one day and 24 hours later you wouldn't want to step in it on the sidewalk. I think that deciding what you want to eat has something to do with your ability to sense how you will feel after you eat it, and how you feel as you get rid of it.

Also, I heard once that every restaurant theme had been tried already, at least that's what I heard some guy on the train say one day and he was in the restaurant business I think because he was wearing a bib. I would be willing to bet though that this idea, one that you and I could do if you want to invest in a restaurant, has never been done. Let's say you have to be really rich to eat at this place, and if you drive up in a car spray-painted primer gray, they turn you away. You also have to dress up and it's very high atmosphere. But the thing is that you sit at a cheap folding table on a folding chair and you get fed wieners by a clown. You can't use any utensils and you have to do what the clown says, like wear a squirrel tail. I don't think that has been done. If I was rich I would go there! Or I would start a restaurant like that for rich people. People who aren't rich can go too, but they enter through another door and get to watch from behind two-way mirrors. This would be cool!

I have some other food ideas too, and if you're interested, let me know. By the way, my mom gets out of the hospital tomorrow.

Bye,

Randy

When wieners are banned,
Someone will still find a way;
Hot dog speakeasy

Dr. Anderson,

That thing I told you about the corn syrup reminded me about the time I worked at a place where our boss was obsessed with stains on the carpet. He knew who made each stain and told you the story about how it got there. Also, the thing all the people who had stained the carpet had in common was this: they didn't work there anymore.

Anyway, he would gaze off in the distance sometimes and start talking about Gary or Sandy, and then you'd know he was looking at the stain on the carpet. It was always from coffee or something. One time I left my coffee under the chair in his office when he was lecturing me about something and I forgot it. Did I tell you this already? Anyway, by the time I remembered where I left my coffee one of his kids who was a salesman there had already knocked over the coffee. I was really glad it was him and not me. I think though that I got some of the blame for it though because it was my coffee. But the kid was the kind of guy that the dad liked to blame for everything that went wrong and you could see the kid was suffering.

I heard one time the the owner's kid got mad and quit. But then he came back a couple of weeks later with all his stuff in a box, so he got his job back. (By the way, that's how you always know someone just got fired because they are carrying a box of stuff around in the city.) One guy I worked with used to always throw all his lunch garbage in the back seat of the kid's car because he would leave the back window open and it was an irresistible invitation. The bosses kid never knew and after about two months the back floor was full of junk and burger wrappers and stuff. I think it was a Lincoln Continental.

I don't know what happened to those people but I always think of the dad in his senior years, floating in a hot tub that's all black and foamy, while his wife scoops out the foam with a net and makes sure none of the tubes get too kinked.

Which reminds me I need another one of those rubber laboratory funnels you sent. My mom will sign for it this time if you use UPS™.

Randy

Dr. Anderson,

I have an idea for the betterment of all of corporate America. I know lately companies have been getting a lot of bad publicity because of the sweatshop thing and even though you'd never believe it could still be happening in America, it is. But it's not really in America and yet American companies are benefit from it.

So anyway it makes me think of the story about the shoemaker and the elves. Can you imagine how it would be to wake up in the morning and find out that elves have been doing all your work at night and they did really great work and you still got to keep all the profits? That is the good thing about the story! They never once say in the moral of the story that you should work hard, and if you need to, you should hire more people to spread around the high wages you could probably afford to pay now that you're selling all those shoes. No, the moral of the story appears to be that if elves come in the night and do all the work you don't have to pay them and you still get to keep all the profits.

So do you think the American people would be as upset as they are by the children working in foreign countries to make American products if the American companies that employed those children just held a press conference? And at the press conference they could just simply state the fact that, no, they aren't children working for hardly any money. They are elves! And they are happy to work for free to make the shoes and the other things that American companies can't make here anymore because high wages would put a big dent in many CEO-retirement plans that involve bass boats and hookers on the high seas. Not that these would be bad things, but it's possible you could fall overboard during your goofing around and then who would be there to give the elves something to do?

I think Americans would be comforted knowing that elves are helping America. In the story of the shoemaker and the elves, we feel better for the shoemaker because he got the free help and it seems okay. So why can't it work for American companies? I think it would work really well. Especially around Christmastime. But I am pretty sure those are a different breed or species of elf. They are like penguin elves because they can stand the cold and take orders from a guy in a red suit. Maybe they are Nordic. Other elves are better adapted to working in hot, sweaty conditions and they probably don't mind having to eat some kind of elf gruel that probably tastes a lot like school paste. I never ate school paste but my friend Bob did and he grew up to be rotund.

Thanks by the way for the buckets!

Randy

El stop at Belmont
Get your army surplus goods
Some Indian food

Dr. Anderson,

I always wondered about this but I never tried to think it all the way through until now, so if it doesn't make any sense it could be because it's the first time I tried to put it all together. And the thing that made me think about this was how many people I see every day who don't know the difference between a good plan and a hunk of cork.

Anyway, the idea I have is this: what if there was a tax for being stupid? The good points of this are as follows: there is a very large number of people to collect tax from; if you worded it right, most of them wouldn't know they were being taxed because they are stupid; you could give them a one percent reduction on their stupid tax for every kid they have. That would encourage them to make more taxable citizens, don't you think?

I figure the tax would be strictly based upon your performance on a test that you had to re-take every five years. And that would be your tax rate. Another good thing is that people who don't want to pay that much tax would get smarter and then they could reduce their tax by becoming more valuable as a citizen.

So you have to take this tax test every five years, and here's another thing that would be good: even if someone is really rich, but really dumb, they would contribute a lot to the country. I know I would have a lot more respect for someone if they figured out how to get rich even though they were (technically) taxably stupid.

The only problem with this is that the people who design the tests would be under a lot of pressure to make the tests passable by stupid rich people. Also I believe another downside to this would be the idea of what is smart would change if there is enough pressure to do it. They might start defining smart not by how many photons you think are in a flashlight beam or what is the life-cycle of a lamprey eel, but by knowing how Kardashians™ reproduce. And on the test, if you correct the spelling of Kardashian Kollection™ you instantly fail. Anyway, that's about as far as I got on that. If you are interested in proposing this to Congress let me know and I'll be happy to write it up so a Senator can read it.

Randy

Dr. Anderson,

I just noted that the Tic Tac™ mint people have a promotion where you collect points from your labels and then you can order stuff from their catalog. I saw they had a Tic Tac™ towel and a Tic Tac™ shirt and a couple of other things but the one that drew my attention was the Tic Tac™ Yahoo!™ digital camera, which leaves me with the unclear impression of whether it is a Tic Tac™ camera or a Yahoo!™ camera. On top of that, it requires you to have 250 Tic Tac™ points. My Tic Tacs™ that I recently got are worth one point. They cost about a dollar if you don't find them on a picnic table in the park like I did.

So, if you spend about 250 dollars on mints, you can get a free camera. Here is the interesting part: If you go to the Yahoo!™ site where they sell Yahoo!™ stuff, you can buy the camera for about 69 dollars. So I just wanted to warn you in case you were about to eat a whole lot of mints so you could get a free camera. One last thing: can you please send me a ringworm brochure?

Thanks,

Randy Scuffle, Chicago patient.

Dr. Anderson,

Remember that time you told me you knew someone who worked at Ticketmaster?™ Could you please send them this letter so I can have my views heard without them being thrown away? Thank you.

Dear Ticketmaster™ or Live Nation™ or whoever you really are,
I have once again become very frustrated by the amount of money you charge for convenience when I can in no way find out what the convenience is when I buy tickets to events. Now that I can buy tickets on the Internet, it's pretty convenient for everybody. Then you charge me for the convenience of it. Who are you people? Do you have employees anywhere who do anything other than count the money? The less work you have to do the more you charge for everything. You must like to be in control.

It all reminds me of how my dad used to make me do tricks before I could eat. I was very hungry and I wanted the food, so I had to do the tricks. One time I had to carry bananas under my arms for about an hour just to get some breakfast, which is okay unless you want bananas on your cereal. I can't eat bananas now. And I don't eat Cheerios™ either. Lucky Charms™ are okay when you're a kid but suddenly you realize that the marshmallows are like chewing the foam backing on some construction materials. Also I never really liked Cap'n Crunch™ because it shredded my mouth. I liked the taste but I also had mouth shreds hanging on my tongue when I got done and they were sometimes as long as a banana stringer and of course you know how I feel about them.

One time my dad made be balance a melon behind my neck for about an hour and then I had to listen to his old marching records. Let me tell you, it is not fun to warm a melon on your neck. Especially when your dinner is only instant macaroni and cheese.

Another thing I'd share with you because it's a little embarrassing is that when you sneeze a hunk of wiener across the room when you are four years old it is stunning to see how many times it bounces before it stops. Oddly, I still like wieners but I can't stand dog hair. Anyway, so now if I want to see a xylophone concert or something and I have no choice but to pay your fees. You should really consider changing this or at least coming up with a better excuse than "convenience." Otherwise, someone will figure out that it is much more fun to meatball your headquarters, which is another problem of mine altogether. But that is not your problem to solve.

Thank you for restoring my hope,

Randy Scuffle
Chicago, Illinois

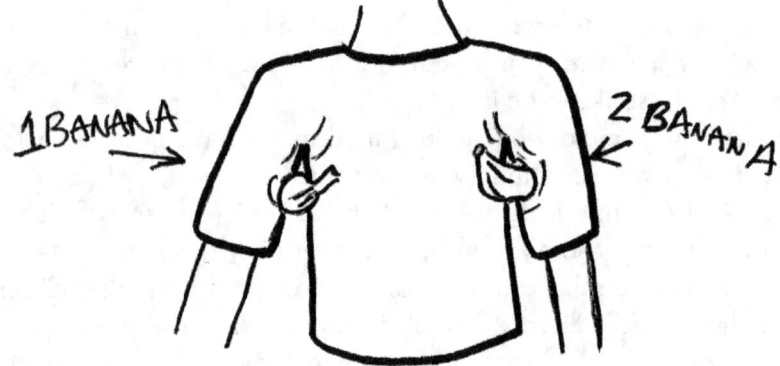

To whom it may concern,

I am responding to your ad in the Chicago Tribune™ for home-based computer support personnel. I have had extensive experience supporting computers and in fact I have a preference for supporting computers over people. I don't really mind talking to the people but quite often they are a little bit difficult. My favorite thing about computers is that they work or they don't work. They don't forget to tell you that they were dropped off a table like users sometimes do.

And then there is the problem of how you get treated by people who need your help, ask for your help, and still treat you like a waiter who just delivered a bunch of dead Lake Michigan alewives on a plate of stinky sand which always ends up somehow in your swimsuit area.

However, I am glad you need people who work out of their homes because that is how I prefer to work. How many phone lines could I get? I am proficient in many technologies and as soon as I learn the basics of a new one I can envision many applications, so I like inventing things and solving problems. I am willing to answer questions for people as long as they are nice to me and it isn't after 8 pm since that is when I do most of my artwork. Yes! I am an artist too. But that is my problem, not yours. I can work around it.

I also want to ask if it is possible to get a vacation even though I work at home. One last thing is that if you ever need people to go out and work on computers, I can do that too but prefer to not have to deal with people who have computers but cannot explain why they do. They seem to be the meanest about how it must be everyone else's fault. Talking to people like that gives me a stomach ache that is usually some kind of gas but not being in my own home I end up being the one who suffers.

Thank you for considering me,

Randy Scuffle, Chicago

Dr. Anderson,

I had a really weird dream last night and it was so vivid and color-ful and filled with dimensions that I have not been the same person since I woke up. In my dream we the people were not the citizens of the United States. The real citizens of the U.S. were Corporations, and we were all Sea Monkeys™ swimming around in these Corporation heads getting things done. We all had specialized jobs exactly like in real life except we were Sea Monkeys™. There were management Sea Monkeys™ and worker Sea Monkeys™ and smart Sea Monkeys™ and lazy Sea Monkeys™ and stupid Sea Monkeys™ and Sea Monkeys™ that didn't have all their parts. Just like in real life.

Also just like in real life, you never knew who was making decisions and when times got bad they would just use fewer Sea Monkeys™. Whenever a company would go out of business, it never seemed to matter. All it did was redistribute the Sea Monkeys™. Then another company would start, oftentimes using some of the same Sea Mon-keys™ to manage it and I guess move around some of its internal parts. The whole thing was very clear: everything exists so that the Corporations can make money and live. Some of the Sea Monkeys™ had really good lives too, if they got to work in special parts of the Corporation, which was shaped just like a head on a shelf somewhere. We were all so tiny that we didn't really know much about the bigger world outside the head, but that didn't matter either since all we cared about was did we get our daily share of brain plaque from the head.

I remember I didn't like the brain plaque I was getting in the vein I worked for a while. Every time I would tear off a hunk of brain plaque it would turn into a picture of Madonna™ or Britney Spears™ or some movie star I never heard of before. Meanwhile, everyone else was just eating their brain plaque and being all happy. It was making me sick to think about biting into Madonna™, and not because I would hurt her face with my teeth and Sea Monkey™ grippers, but because she was made out of some kind of chemically smelling stuff that had been injected with lots of air and spiders.

So all the other Sea Monkeys™ in my group were happily chewing and chewing and chewing and they were still losing weight because there was no nutrition in the Madonna™ brain plaque, which by now in my dream had turned into an olive loaf rabbit. The Britney Spears™ heads were just as bad only the insides were really dry. But it was the only food we had, and that was the really bad part. The more you looked for good brain plaque the more energy you had to use and so you *had* to eat the Madonna™ heads so you had enough energy to find the rare good ones. I was in this one artery for a while where all the other Sea Monkeys™ were really fat and lazy and gross looking and the brain plaque heads looked a lot like Matthew Lesko™, that guy who tries to get you to buy a book that tells you the same things you can get for free from the government if you write to some address in Pueblo, Colorado. But he charges for it and wears a bright green jacket filled with question marks, which just fills my head with question marks about why this guy makes so much money selling people what they can get for free, which then just makes me think again about America Online™ and I get frustrated and end up making a wiener sandwich and taking a nap.

By the way, I heard about this place in Berwyn called Big Guys Sausage™. If it's as good as everyone says, I will need a new battery for the golf cart. A day trip would be good for my essence. I will let you know!

Randy

Dear Uncle Andy,

My doctor said it would be a good idea to write you a letter to tell you some things about how I am doing since the accident with the turpentine. He said I would feel better to tell you about my feelings related to that time you put the cigarette butt out on my head. Even though I was only three I think it made an impression on me. I thought you were a good uncle even though you burned my hair. My mom thought it was from a sparkler that we had because she hit Larry for doing it to me. I don't remember if I had a scab on my head or not because I was only three, but I remember you putting your cigarette out on my head. Once about five years ago I told my Mom that you did it and she said the only way you would ever have done that would be if you were drunk on Old Style™ again. But I don't remember if you were drunk because I was only three.

I also remember the time you drove me and Larry around in your new Mustang. It was cool and fast. My mom says you drive like a jerk when you are drunk on Blatz™ but I don't remember you drunk. I think I was nine and Larry was eleven maybe. What happened to that car? I never remember it after that. I remember the time we blew off whole rolls of caps with a hammer on a tree stump. I remember I did get a scab on my hand from when you made me hold the caps on the stump. I'm sorry you got in trouble. The scab fell off in about a week and my thumbnail grew back too.

That time your friend Gary Roberts gave me the Old Milwaukees™ under the bridge was about the same time that Mom came home with you in the police car. Did they run the siren? Was it loud? I'm sorry you got blamed for that, but Mom made me tell or she would have probably cried in her room for about a day again.

My mom said once that your mom used to bite you in the arm a lot if you were bad. And here all along I thought maybe you got hit with a lot of baseballs during practice or something. My doctor says it was probably not normal that your mom bit you. One time I accidentally saw your mom without her bra on. She kept looking at me and I didn't want to get bit, so I ran. That's when I got the black eye from the door but you thought I got punched by Eddie. I'm sorry I saw your mom naked. Here's a funny thing, Uncle Andy, I don't really think about your mom as being my grandma. She seems so unrelated to me. Anyway, I'm sorry you can't come visit us this year. My mom says you're still working on the farm. Every time I get an apple or a carrot I think you grew it. My mom also says you need help. Bye!

Randy

Official Draft List of Responses to Various Actions Against the USA

Proposed List of New War Rules

Drafted by Randall Scuffle, Chicago

If Your Country:	We will:
Kidnaps an American	Dump cabbage on you (we have lots of cabbage and not everything gets used when making sauerkraut)
Plots to blow up our stuff	Dump perfume inserts on you (Your land will smell terrible and you will be unable to enjoy flowers)
Blows up our stuff	Dump used baby diapers on you (Your land will smell terrible and we enjoy a cleaner landscape for our future generations)
Attacks us	Dump last week's ground beef on you (These will attract flies which will also go for the diapers that we already dropped on you.)

Dear Dr. Anderson,

My mom insists I write to you about something she is worried about. She is concerned about the soup I make with wieners. It's good. I'll give you the recipe. She says there are no good food qualities in wiener soup. I say there are plenty and proof of that is that I am alive and functioning just fine. So far in the past month I have made wiener soup every day and I feel great.

The other night she came out here into the yard and started crying about how just eating wiener soup all the time will make me translucent and I will have no tone to my fibers. She wants me to put vitamins in the soup. I don't really care about the vitamins because I think they add a metal flavor to the soup.

Oh, here is the recipe: Take a pot of rainwater and boil it on the fire. Then add a pack of wieners, being careful to first remove the plastic wrapping. Boil the wieners in the water until it looks like soup. Usually about two hours. Eat and smile.

She says there is not enough in there to keep me going. I'm fine. I'm working on a new project too. She's just mad because of the foil on the windows. My new project is probably going to be seen in many newspapers and on television. You'll be glad you know me because it will ensure my fame as an artist.

This entire fall season I'm going to live in the backyard and eat wiener soup. That's my project! The best part is that no one will know I'm me the artist doing the performance, they will all believe I hired an actor or a mime to wear the clown suit. That way I can observe my own anonymity first hand and still enjoy the fame. I don't want anyone to know about this though until about a month into the project, since newspapers don't run to your house the first day you declare your intentions.

Anyway, I will let you know how the wiener soup project is going. If you want a batch, let me know and I'll have my mom bring you a jug of it. Do you want one wiener in it or two?

Randy Scuffle

Dr. Anderson,

I was watching the Sea Monkeys™ this morning and they are growing well. I'm sure I told you about my Sea Monkey™ and Ryan Seacrest™ theory, so I won't go into that again, except to note that I have finally addressed the problem with changing the nesting heads without losing too much of the nutrient goo. I don't think it's worth patenting just yet.

Yesterday my notebook of train numbers filled up, and the last train number in it is 3336. I'm thinking of putting these in a database so I can find patterns of which cars come by at the same time each day, but it is highly dependent on which car I get in since that is the only car number I ever write down. So far I have ridden in the same numbered car on several occasions and I wonder if I have a better day based on the number of the car, or whether or not it has a softer ride.

So far my theory of trains boils down to knowing that on the Red Line the air conditioning never works and it is pretty stale. The Purple Line can go either way, with air or without. The Brown Line almost always has air conditioning even when it is cold outside. The only exception to this rule is when it is about 95 outside and you get in a car that has the heat on. That is not good, and everyone inside looks like they are filled with hot, over-cooked macaroni. No one is happy, and then Old Wood Hand starts yelling about waiting for about an hour for the train and now she will be cooked alive.

Last time I saw her she had a new haircut and she painted the nails on her wood hand blue or purple. I couldn't tell because I didn't want to stare at her the way people sometimes stare when I am in a clown phase of my research. She can hold a cigarette in it, and it of course made me think of what would she do if she went to take a puff and it turned out to be a wiener that got stuck in there after being shot out of the improved wiener rocket during a wiener storm.

I also bet that if I put a foil ball in each wiener before I loaded the gun you could track the storm on Doppler™ radar. After the storm I could call the Air Force to see if they saw the wiener storm in Chicago on their radar. I need to stir the monkeys now, so I have to go.

Randy

Dr. Anderson,

I can't believe how often this occurs to me. I think a lot about how children and dogs are very good potential hosts for parasites. They are both low to the ground and they both play in the dirt a lot. Both of them have been known to scoot across the carpet and both are also unable to tell you when they feel like something is living in them. Kids and dogs also have a tendency to put a lot of things in their mouths. Dogs do it because they don't have hands. Kids do it because their mouths are their most sophisticated sensory organ besides whatever gland it is that makes that yellow cream my cousin Amy saw in her kid's diaper. It really smells bad too, and I don't know how she can ever get it off her hands.

One time we were at her house and one of her kids came out holding a piece of cake and it had cake in its hair and it had cake all over its shirt and it wasn't wearing any pants. It offered me some cake but I also noticed that the child was surrounded by a smell that couldn't have been chocolate even in a negative universe like the one I saw on *Star Trek* a long time ago. And speaking of that I can't tell you how many times I worry that I'm sitting on a booger on the train.

Yesterday I was on car 3406 and I'm very glad I lined these pants with the foil. It was about 99 degrees on the train and at least that protected me from any reconstitution of booger meat that might want to dig through my pants and infect me with a pinworm or something. I'm way too old to have my mom rooting around with a flashlight at night.

Oh, one other thing about dogs is that you can just go to the store and buy an anti-parasite medicine and you and the dog are both happy. But when your kid gets worms you feel ashamed for letting something crawl up inside of it and make a new home.

I am ready to talk about the other stuff soon.

Randy

Dear Dr. Anderson,

Randy won't come out of the backyard! He put up the pup tent about a month ago and started sleeping outside. Then I couldn't get him out of the yard except for food time. But then he started only eating wieners and buns. I was okay with that for about two weeks because at least he was eating again. About a week later he would only eat them if I cooked them on a stick over the flames of the stove. Now he has a campfire in the yard and cooks everything out there. At first I thought this was just another Boy Scout phase but even when he was a Scout he ate more than just wieners. He cooks the wieners on a stick with a nail in it that he got from when his father had things in the garage. The buns he holds over the flames or he sometimes just throws them on a hot rock.

I'm worried about two things. What if he burns himself; will it heal if he won't come out of the yard? I asked him what will he do if he burns himself on the fire because he says he won't leave the yard anymore. He says, and I'm not a doctor so I don't know if this is true, but he says you can just rub wiener juice on burns and they heal faster than if you go to the doctor.

The other thing that worries me is if he's getting all the vitamins he can get from the wieners. I read once where they don't have all the nutrition for kids or anyone else. Can you write him a note about this? I will bring it to him next time I deliver his mail just like always. I hope he doesn't think wiener juice will be the next cure-all or we're going to have more bills like we did after the sewer grate incident. I still wonder if that puppy could really talk.

Thank you,

Phyllis Scuffle

Dr. Anderson,

The Sea Monkeys™ are not working out as I had hoped. They are willful and disobedient. I raised them and trained them and now they just sit there staring at me like I am supposed to do something. It's really kind of spooky when you think about how close they are to my head when I sleep at night. Last night I had this thought that if I did get them to eat brain plaque and they did the job properly they wouldn't have much to eat and then what? I can't imagine Ryan Seacrest™ being able to host some show knowing that at any moment the Sea Monkeys™, dispatched to help him live forever, might actually attack his brain or, worse yet, the Hollywood-caulk that must hold him together.

Anyway, my mom was right about the bomb shelter. I found it when I was looking for a place to dump some bad wiener soup that somehow got feathers in it. I don't think my mom knows I found it though. She has been knitting a set of curtains for her room and they are almost finished. She hardly ever plays the organ anymore, not since her one foot swelled up and out of the slipper that gave her the best pedal-grip. She says her foot is too hard and it slides on the pedals, so I sprayed some sticky stuff on them from this can. It worked for about a week until the sticky stuff had collected all the dust that was under the organ.

Now her toes get furry when she plays, and she claims to be allergic to dust. The first day was the worst because everywhere she walked she had things stick to her. She came outside though for the first time in about 3 months so I could pick off the fuzz for her. That made me think maybe she needed some new slippers. If you don't know what kind she had and can't get her some more Dr. Anderson, I was wondering if she could use some bologna slippers. I would make them more like shower thongs so her feet could breathe. Also, you could keep the weight down with olive loaf shoes, because the olives would fall out and you would get more air circulation to your feet. I'm not sure how grippy they would be though on the organ. I will run some tests first. By the way, the bomb shelter still has electricity hooked up and everything.

Randy

Dr. Anderson,

There was a bubbling sensation today in my mind as I realized that the wiener rocket idea has a lot of potential during the holidays. Imagine if you can the artistic beauty of wieners being shot into the air during the fireworks display on the 4th of July. If that isn't enough, imagine that each one exploded when it reached its highest point in the air. In my brain I keep hearing a dull, muffled popping noise of the wiener explosions, only to be followed by that bubbling sensation I was telling you about when I think about all the wiener meat raining down on the crowd. Maybe I could even put messages inside of them that people would want to read. This would be a good way to distribute my urban haikus I told you about. This one would be good:

> Summer hot dog meat
> Rain showers from the night sky;
> Boom! Spider flowers

Meanwhile, I have lost another bucket of Sea Monkeys™. It was too hot this summer to raise them and keep them in training. I could tell there was going to be trouble when they became disoriented and feckless at around 100 degrees. You can only stir them so much and then they just give up and turn to sludge. It's sad that they used to be such a happy family but now they are in the garden. I suppose that's good because next year they will come back as flowers or even those weeds that you think are going to be flowers and then all of a sudden they grow prickly things and release all that fuzzy stuff that sticks to your lips in the morning.

One time when I was a kid my Uncle Andy made me eat milkweed pods because he said they were the same as okra but my mouth went numb on one side and I got a blister on my tongue. That wasn't so bad but going to the bathroom was hard for about a week. The doctor said my mom should have brought me in earlier to get something pumped out but it was really too late since I digest things pretty fast. Except for the milkweed silk. Anyway, after that Andy never came over again and my mom said he went to work on a farm again for a while.

I have to go wake my mom up now so she can watch for traffic. Monday was pretty muddy, so now we have more ruts in the front yard.

Randy Scuffle

A perfect morning in Scottsdale, AZ with the Wienermobile reflecting sky and palm trees. I could almost smell the soup. Another sighting in the wild!

Dr. Anderson,

I learned one thing this weekend: no matter how much you beat a hot dog with a hammer, it never looks the same as when you chew it. Also I found out that the ones you bounce off the house after being shot from the wiener rocket will break but they don't smash up as you would expect. I have not yet experimented with the idea of skinning a wiener by shooting it at a sand dune, which I could do in Indiana if my mom would take me there without yelling about the rocket sticking out of the back of the car. She says it is dangerous for the barrel to be hanging out like that but I told her about the law that says you have to have something red hanging from it anyway so that people driving behind you don't get a wiener barrel in their windshields.

If you send more caulk and one of those clamps that I got last year for Christmas from my mom then I can probably do the ultimate thing that I have always wanted to do. Oh, and I'll also need two more scuba tanks and a welding regulator too. I went scuba diving once and all I saw on the bottom of the lake was murk and a few dead fish that had heads and no eyes but their bodies were all bones from being picked at by turtles and crabs. I think that's the same thing that happened to that rich guy who used to run the publishing company in England and after some mishap on his boat he was found a few days later all bloated in the ocean.

I don't think that would be a good way to go, but my real fear has always been that I would be found dead with my pants down because for some reason our house blew up while I was in the bathroom. It really bothered me for a long time and then I figured I just had to hurry up and not stay in there too long. Besides, my mom always says if you read on the toilet you'll get piles, so there are two reasons not to waste time in there. I don't think we ever had a gas problem in the house though. At least not that kind of gas.

Anyway, my ultimate design will require the scuba tanks filled with air and I can then mount a modified wiener rocket on the front of our car. Then when you are behind a white SUV and the driver is on the phone and double parking and driving like they have only one arm and a really short leg, you can blow hamburger all over the back of the SUV. I think that would be nice. And hard to clean.

If you want to invest in the wiener rocket, I bet we could make lots of money selling it to people stuck behind SUVs in traffic all day. This would also be good for the meat industry since they would be able to expand their market to the hamburger blasters. Also when there is a listeria outbreak and they have to recall a million pounds of meat we can just packet them up into blaster packs and sell them. By the time you get them they would be ripe and ready for blasting.

Now if we really want to make a lot of money we hook up a template of some kind in front of the gun like when you play with those dough toys that come out in shapes, but this way the burger blast makes a painting on the SUV or maybe it spells out something like DORK or something. Let me know what you want to do, I think we'd have to set up a corporation based in Florida and do an infomercial. I think the perfect guy would be that man who wears the green suit with the question marks on it who tells people his name is Matthew Lesko.

Randy

Three in the morning;
Two char-dogs with hot peppers
One Wieners Circle

Dr. Anderson,

Please send more duct tape, a packet of spigots and one of those medium sized hoses, preferably green. I figured out how to adapt the logic from my old printer and use it to make the meat spray say whatever you want it to. I have to experiment with typing while driving but as long as my mom doesn't stop in the middle of an intersection I should be okay with that. So far I have made it spray out short words but not with meat, only with paint. Next I will try something more gooey like dough or something. I don't want to clog up the meat writer before I get a chance to really try it out.

My mom will probably be writing to you soon about how the house now has a bunch of dots on the side; I needed something to practice with. She doesn't know that if you stand back about 10 feet it says "flub," but that's how it works when you work in meat dots. I also think this would be a good way to attract flies to the SUVs that you anoint. Most of those girls with the blonde pony tails and the baseball caps don't like to swat flies when they get into their SUVs; otherwise they can't work the key, the latte, and the phone at the same time.

If the meat writer project gets the funding that I think it should, you will see many SUVs with various words ghosted into the paint, because I bet that even after you wash off the meat it still looks a lot like the paper under your Italian beef. I stopped eating those after the incident with the hot peppers. I had to wear sunglasses halfway through 6th grade.

I have to go wash out the test tubes before the crust sets.

Randy Scuffle, Chicago patient (improving)

Dr. Anderson,

I saw where a furniture store lets you buy stuff but not pay until two years from now. I was thinking you and your legal friends could help me get together this idea so we could all make a bunch of money. Here is the idea: What if you never had to pay for anything until after you died? What if you could just buy stuff and say put it on my account, and then it all comes out of your life insurance after you're dead? I think that would be great, except you'd have to make sure the creditors got extra interest or something and they would agree to do that. How will we make money? I haven't figured that out yet.

By the way, it is impossible to tattoo your tongue with a pen like they do in prison. The ink keeps washing off. No matter how much time I spend panting, it keeps getting wet. I've tried to limit my liquid intake too, just to experiment. Last week I filled up a quart jar with saliva after about three hours. I don't know if that's normal output, but I'm using it as my baseline. Then I tried to see what happened if I didn't drink water for a couple of days, but it just made the saliva look more drinkable. Then I tried putting food I don't like in front of me, like fish sticks. That also kept the output down. Then I had my mom hang a hot dog out the window on a fishing line. My drool output was very consistent and I filled up the jar again.

Unfortunately, the grass was wet and the clown pants stuck to me pretty bad, especially after I stood up and had to pull them out from where my tail would still be if it had not evolved off before I was born. Let me know about the insurance idea. I will think about it too...

Randy

Dr. Anderson,

My son Randy is acting up again. His briefcase is still leaning against the fence even though he says he's been going to work. I don't think he has been following any of your advice, and now I'm afraid he might try to dig more tunnels. I see him hanging around the bushes sometimes, but he has done that ever since he was a child. I remember when he got all full of hives from rubbing the raspberries on himself. At first I thought the bees had returned but I had thrown out all his orange shirts, so I didn't figure it out until I noticed the berry streaks. That was pretty easy to handle compared to the wood chip incident. It took about two weeks for the splinters to pass.

Anyway, Randy said last week that he wanted to live like a mole for the winter, which is at least admirable if you are a mole, but he is not. His baby picture makes him look all squinty but that is because he is working on some kind of project no doubt.

Could you please call someone to come and get the bologna blocks out of the yard? Last winter the squirrels and birds made a big mess out of everything, and someone tried to climb the bird feeder pole, which is now kind of bent to one side so that all the sunflower seeds fall out of the feeder. Please talk some sense into him.

Oh, and the other thing I wanted to know was what to do with these checks that have started coming for Randy. I'll send them to you if you want me to. Just put them in whichever account is best for now.

Thanks a lot, Dr. Anderson,

Phyllis Scuffle
Randy Scuffle's mother

Dr. Anderson,

Last year at this time I was much colder. The tent worked okay but I needed so many duffel bags filled with towels to keep in the heat that I couldn't really move around much. So to solve all that I've moved into the bomb shelter. You'll be happy to know that the computers also work much better in the shelter, especially without dried leaves stuck in the fans, which reminded me of this old car we had but I can't remember what it was (it might have been the Buick because that had a good blower even in summer).

Anyway, in fall a whole bunch of leaves would get into the slotted area between the windshield and the hood of the car. Then when they dried out, the first time you turned on the heater in winter little chunks of leaves would blow out all over the inside of the car. It was dusty and then everything crunched in the car and I had to show up at my cousin's wedding with leaf-stems in my hair. I got most of them out except for the big one that wedged its way into a couple of stitches on my head from the tussle with the feral cat. Luckily it didn't maul the yarn wig. I still don't trust cats unless they are asleep or in someone else's yard.

By the way, thanks for the extra dirt; it will help even more this winter. I extended the bomb shelter entry hatch with that old culvert pipe from the garage that my dad saved after the fire department had to cut it in half. That was a long day! The shoes make it a little hard to walk up and down the ladder, but it is kind of funny to hear the noise they make on the culvert ridges. The other thing is that the Sea Monkey™ project is just about dead. Most of them escaped and they ate my art project depicting the second president Bush. I don't know why they only ate that one, but now he is just a nub.

I have to go now. Let me know if you like shrimp.

Randy

Dr. Anderson,

Honestly, the meat-writer is not working like I want it to, and instead of looking like someone wrote a message in neat letters it looks more like hamburger-stucco. I could use it to coat someone's house if they wanted to be part of an art project, but someone at the Art Institute has beaten me to a similar idea by growing an army of flies.

Can you send some more of those little picture frames that look like they are expensive but they are not? I like the deeper ones because I have this idea that involves them and cocktail wieners. The only problem is with seepage and the wiener juice soaks into the backing. I tried something less absorbent, and ended up with all the juice at the bottom. You know those frames filled with nails that you can stick you face into and it pokes out an image of you but it's in nails, not in paint? It works with wieners instead of the nails, especially with cocktail franks and the smoky ones. The only time it doesn't work really well is if you have a very big nose or a chin bigger than a clamshell. In that case you have to use full-sized wieners. And then you get the nose-depth but you lose the resolution because of the wiener thickness.

So that led me to a better idea, which requires a really big frame bigger than me, maybe from a door or something. Full-sized wieners would give you adequate resolution if you were going to do the whole body, not just the face. If I apply my soon-to-be-patented Bolognafication™ process to the wieners maybe this would work. Plus, it wouldn't attract the flies and then the critics couldn't say it was derivative of the work previously done at the Art Institute.

Anyway, if I get several door frames and make them into 3D wiener art boxes, I can set them up around a room and have poses of me depicting 12 stages of my life. This project is the ultimate, Dr. Anderson. I'm sure it would be a good thing for anyone who appreciates my projects. You know the art critics are getting more and more selective about what they decide is meaningful, so if you could, please ask one of your friends at the museum if I can rent out a room for a show. I think I am ready.

Randy Scuffle

Dr. Anderson,

I'm concerned that there are no new ideas for sitcoms. It seems like if you have watched TV for a while you realize that it's the same stories over and over but with different shows and characters playing them out. Just to give you an example, I know for a fact that both *The Dick Van Dyke Show* and *Gilligan's Island* shared the same story about someone becoming accidentally hypnotized. How often does that happen? I think it is more interesting to see what characters do in different situations, but maybe there is a shortage of situations.

Maybe people are so used to seeing only these same situations over and over again that they don't think anymore about how even in their own lives they do things that are never shown on situation comedies. And this is weird to me, since everyone seems to feel they can identify with their favorite characters and shows, yet they never do anything that happens in real life. I don't wish my life was like anyone's on TV, except maybe for that one guy who always sells carpet on Channel 9. I bet his house is soft.

I used to be able to roll around on the floor or the carpets until that one Christmas with the double-stick tape episode and my mom's bird Grippy. I guess that's another thing I can't talk about much, but sometimes she sings the Grippy song, which she made up and has since learned to play on the organ. The only words I remember are "Grippy when you're wet, Grippy when you're dry, Grippy like a headache, oh Grippy can you fly."

Then that gets in my head like other songs I told you about before and the next thing I know I'm on the bus and I can't figure out why some man singers sound like girl singers. It makes my brain go numb and robs me of better ideas. Why are women attracted to men who sing like girls? Anyway, when she talks about the bird then I can remember him too. I think he would have liked living in the yard.

Randy

Dr. Anderson,

I have been thinking more and more about my dream city and how I would build it. There would have to be laws, but it is my city so I can make up the laws, like when my mom used to say as long as I am living under her roof I have to eat the cabbage rolls. So here are the rules I have so far for my city. I figure that if anyone doesn't like it they can live somewhere else, like Oshkosh or any other city along Lake Winnebago. Here are the rules so far:

1. The city council must work for the citizens and they must report to us regularly.
2. The city council can never vote on some new law that none of us have ever heard of before or that we didn't request.
3. The city council may not vote themselves or anyone else a raise.
4. If you want to send junk mail to anyone in my city (I have to come up with a name for it, and I think request an official zip code), you must pay an extra fee that helps pay for garbage pickup.
5. If you want to drive a car in the city you must pay $500 per year to register it in the city.
6. There will be no parking meters.
7. Anyone who wants to drive an SUV in the city must paint it pink with white dots and it has to have a picture of a clown somewhere on it.
8. Anyone who drives an SUV in the city must pull to the curb when a smaller vehicle approaches from the rear. As the smaller vehicle passes, the driver of the SUV must wave to the passing vehicle and say "I'm sorry," in a sincere, polite manner. Especially Hummers™, regardless of size.
9. People of all kinds are welcome, but stupid people who make a lot of money must wear a badge that says "Hello, I'm rich and stupid."
10. Any person of wealth, who drinks excessively, runs other people over with their car or SUV, and then tries to capi-

talize on the fame gained from the incident, must pay the city and the injured person's family $10 million each.

11. Any business that prefers to cater to the wealthy shall pay the city a big chunk of money each year (I don't know how much yet). The amount will be larger if the business tries to exclude other citizens from entering, or somehow discriminates against people who aren't investment bankers or whose fathers don't own publishing companies or candy companies. So for example a restaurant that you can only get into if you are famous will pay a lot. (And will donate meat for auctions and art fairs.)

12. If the city spends money on making something nice, like a really nice lawn in a park, the croquet and lawn bowling clubs do not have the right to argue over which group gets to use it. The city paid for it, so everyone can use it. If the clubs want to rent an area from the city and pay to have the lawn made nice, they can do that. But the city will rent them a junky area so they can fix it up nice.

13. I will probably be the mayor in the beginning despite my aversion to politics.

14. We declare that citizens of this city are not merely target markets. Therefore, any company that wants to advertise to citizens of my city must pay a licensing fee to each citizen. In exchange for the right to advertise to us, we agree to pay more attention. This applies to television, radio, newspapers, all outdoor advertising and logos on clothes.

15. Streets may be named for companies and or products but the company must pay an annual licensing fee to the city as part of a long-term agreement. The company "adopting" a street will also pay for all maintenance of that street through the duration of the agreement with the city. Additionally, any product or company name deemed "stupid" or "unpronounceable" by the citizens of the city must pay even more by a factor determined by dice roll.

16. Failure by a company to comply with the maintenance agreement on their street, after an unanswered warning by the city, will result in the city renaming the street. After

one warning, "Disney™" street for example, just to pull a name out of a hat, will be named "Dirty Disney™" street. After two warnings, "Disgusting Disney™" street. After three warnings "Don't Shop At Disney™" street. After that, we can do whatever we want.

17. Whenever possible, the city will avoid issuing construction contracts to the lowest bidder as a matter of principle. My city will not be built by the lowest bidder, like much of the U.S. has been.

18. Any citizen who doesn't shovel the snow off their sidewalk because they are afraid to be sued because the act of shoveling somehow shows liability, shall be sued by the city immediately. The citizen must also choose between a sign on their front lawn that says "I'm lazy and stupid," or a sign on their front lawn that says "I'm stupid and lazy."

19. Any citizen who tries to reserve a parking space after a snowstorm by placing chairs or other objects in the street shall be neutered.

20. Any homeowners insurance company that wants to do business in our city shall pay up in the event that something really major happens. We're not going to be stupid enough to put our city right on a river, you know.

21. Anyone who commits a crime in our city using a gun will go to jail. And if that person says something stupid like "I didn't mean for the gun to go off," or "I am a victim of my childhood," will still go to jail. But they can't appeal their sentence until they write a letter of apology to everyone in town. The city will supply the pens and paper.

22. Women who wear baseball caps, sweatshirts bearing the name of any university, and long lycra or similar leg coverings, shall be licensed by the city. The women must display their license tag whenever they go out dressed like that. A special stamp must be purchased at a cost of an extra $25 if she wants to wear her baseball cap backwards.

23. Men wearing baseball caps backwards shall pay a fine of $25. Two men together wearing backwards baseball caps shall pay a fine of $50 each. Three men together wearing

backwards baseball caps shall pay a fine of $100 each. Four or more men together wearing backwards baseball caps shall pay a fine of $1000 each. Fines are not applicable if offenders can prove they are major league baseball catchers.

24. Any number of men wearing baseball caps backwards yelling "skin to win" or "show us your tits" shall be forced to walk home with no pants, in addition to the above fines.

25. Any man or woman wearing a backwards baseball cap shall, in addition to all other fines outlined above, pay the following *additional* fees as indicated if they are:
    a. in an SUV, $100;
    b. near a dog with a bandana around its neck, $100;
    c. talking on a cellphone, $100;
    d. talking on a cellphone, Bluetooth™ in ear, $200;
    e. talking on a cellphone, Bluetooth™ in ear, while in an SUV and with a dog that has a bandana around its neck, $10,000.

26. Anyone (regardless of title or position) who opens a closing elevator door so they can get in, thereby delaying the other passengers shall make amends by one of the following methods, determined by the other passengers:
    a. apologize and then tell a joke;
    b. apologize and sing a song;
    c. apologize and give everyone else in the elevator $50;
    d. all of the above

That's all I have for now. I'm sure there is more coming.

Randy

Dr. Anderson,

I was eating lunch the other day at this place that lets you stay and eat without having to talk to anyone dressed as an animal or a barbershop quartet guy, and I realized that something was making me crazy. I kept hearing someone chewing their food and there was no one really that close to me. I looked for the combination of jaw moving and chewing noises and I finally found a match. This guy was eating like a dog with peanut butter in its mouth and he was dropping food out of his mouth all over the place. It made my hot dog seem less appealing and that is the first time in my life that I ever felt that way about a hot dog.

Then I realized I had become obsessed with his chewing. Not obsessed like when I first came to see you about the clicking and hopping but more like when you can't stop looking at a certain color of marker on the bus seat, and how it blends in at the edges because it was almost out of ink when someone wrote their name. I saw a woman once who looked like a regular person take out a big fat marker and write her name on the train window when she thought no one was looking. I thought she was someone's mom but she was also a graffiti artist I guess. So in a way I can feel like we have something in common.

My art though doesn't include writing my name on everything. I don't even sign my own sculptures because then someone will figure out how to make copies. Once that happens there is no turning back. I have only once put my name on my art; I put my name in a little box behind the pimento of the olive-eye of the Presidential bologna sculpture. I thought it would add another level to the art experience in that only I would know that the President had my name so close to his brain. I like to watch him on TV talking and I imagine that, if his eye was really my olive and he was my talking meat sculpture, that he would be only one blink away from knowing my name.

Also for the dark side of my mind there is the level of art that happens because he couldn't see my name to read it due to the fact that it is behind his eye instead of in front of it. If I was really small I could be in that box and come out when he is giving a speech and maybe climb on his optic nerve or something and pull on it so he sees stars or maybe starts to stare off into space for a minute.

That would be great art, but I am much bigger than that. I also have this fear that once your name is in the President's mind you are on some kind of list that they download out of the back of his neck at the end of the day. I think it is a HDMI connection or something that they use for video. As long as they don't pump electricity into his head then any active Sea Monkeys™ would probably be okay, but lately I'm pretty convinced this project will not happen. Most of them escaped as I told you before, and the one batch I found was all clumped together by a post. That was the batch that pretty much had no leader. They were very obedient and I don't know how they escaped, unless they leaked out of their bucket when I left that spigot open that one time.

The other batch I have not found yet. They are the most dangerous of the Sea Monkeys™ because they were all pretty strong and they seemed to have developed the ability to allow one or more Sea Monkeys™ to lead them. When I first saw that, it became clear that the foreman would be the one I had to persuade to lead the others into Ryan Seacrest's™ head to clean out the plaque. Of course, that venture fell through because Ryan Seacrest™ never returned my offers to help him live forever. He might have signed an agreement with someone else. So now I am waiting to hear from Donald Trump™.

Anyway, as I was watching this guy eat at the restaurant, I realized that except for the fact that he was only half as hairy as a dog, he was just like an animal, but an animal that knew how to find a place to sit down and eat. So I left, and now I am worried that I might just be an animal that knows how to type. I have to go again. By the way, the clown-pant flap idea worked really well.

Thanks!
Randy

Dr. Anderson,

Could you please put together a legal proposal for a patent I hope to obtain? If you talk to our lawyer he will actually do the legal part, but I know you will want to help on some of the wording. Anyway, I'm really excited about this new idea I have but I want to make sure we get the patent before anyone else does. My idea is this: I read about gene splicing and recombinant DNA and I think I can figure out how to create a living hot dog.

The idea is to use the casing as the cell membrane, but inject a newly formed life form into it that I would create here in the lab in my yard. Once I bring a hot dog to life, there will be many good things that come from it. First, I would select the best swimmers and breed more of them. I would then sell these "aqua-dogs" to the Department of Natural Resources in Wisconsin, Vermont or other states. They can stock ponds and rivers with them, and you can go fishing for hot dogs instead of trout or other rare fish.

This would also allow the seafood industry to make a comeback provided I come up with a saltwater, ocean-going version of the aqua-dogs. I can envision whole wiggly nets full of them being caught in choppy seas around the world. This of course depends on making sure they are all good breeders, which is one trait I would ensure existed in all varieties. I can start the breeding program right here using buckets.

Also, I would probably want a land-bound hot dog that would like to live in the woods. I think it would be better for them to sleep in the trees and not on the ground otherwise deer and bears would hunt them down. A trait to avoid in these "terra dogs" would be a pack mentality, because with their ability to breed so fast they would try to take over a whole town or at least try to cross airport runways all at once, slowing traffic to a halt. I don't think it would be a good idea to fly a 787 Dreamliner™ through a pack of terra-dogs.

Which raises an ethical issue regarding this whole thing: the wiener companies wouldn't have to kill animals anymore to make hot dogs, since they would reproduce as hot dogs. But, you'd have to devise a very good test to prove that the hot dogs are as dumb as plants, or there may be protesters trying to save the hot dogs from being eaten.

Worse yet, someone may try to give them the right to vote. If that happens, you'll see really weird commercials during election years. Anyway, think about this and let me know what you want to do. By the way, the new stereo microscope is great!

Randy Scuffle

Chicago patient

PROTOTYPE
TERRA - DOG

Dr. Anderson,

It's been raining so much again lately that I didn't even notice the giant puffball mushroom that had grown in the corner by the fence where I keep my bucket of bologna carving tools has returned. This thing is so big you could play tether-ball with it, but I'm pretty sure that the chain would either pull out of the mushroom or my fist would tear it apart before you could get much of a game in.

Besides, you don't really want to play with food otherwise there will be problems with your digestive system. At least that's what my mom always said happened to my cousin Doug after he ate the PlayDoh™ and started burping about a hundred times in a row. I couldn't believe how many times you could burp without really taking time for more air. I think it was red PlayDoh™ too, so Doug thought it was cherry or maybe raspberry. He was in the hospital for a day and said that when it came out it was still the same color, so it must not have mixed with any other colors otherwise it would have come out brown. My mom says Doug was stupid for eating it.

Anyway I found out there is a big art festival coming and I think I could be the only one there with bologna-art sculptures. One really good one would be for me to create a whole bunch of famous actors and put them in a jury box. Then I could call it "Hollywood on Trial™" or "Jury of My Fears™," or something like that, but the jury box would be filled with bologna actors (but not flies because I want this display to last). I will have to be strict about the soon-to-be-patented Bolognafication™ process. So far my list of people includes Richard Simmons and Bea Arthur. Mainly I am choosing people based on the qualification that I have had dreams about them and that they scare me. And they are actors or at least somehow famous, even if dead.

I know I told you about my Bea Arthur dream, Dr. Anderson. I've often wondered what the whole thing is really about because she is not like my mom and she is not like a woman I would be interested in, since she is obviously not a pigeon-toed redhead.

Randy Scuffle

Dr. Anderson,

I'm getting stronger feelings that I should go with the bologna actors in a jury box since last night I think I ate too many pineapple slices and almost dreamed my head off. This one was very interesting and featured the return of Richard Simmons to my dreams, but this time it was Richard coming over to my house and telling my mom to not make him fight with that Matthew Lesko guy.

So in the dream Richard Simmons is almost crying and begging my mother to not make him have the slap-fight, and my mom says she doesn't know what he is talking about but asks him anyway how many calories are in turkey skin. Then my mom says it's all my fault and then he starts coming after me with these playing cards that have fish and bread on them. It's just like those card-matching games we used to play when I was at camp but instead of matching authors or famous art you have to match up food parts and build your meals.

He says over and over that he doesn't want to fight Matthew Lesko. And the whole time his pasty legs look all dwarfed by his giant socks and cartoon size shoes. It's really weird don't you think? So now I can't get over this idea that Matthew Lesko and Richard Simmons both have to be in the jury box of bologna actors that I present at the art fair. I will put Matthew Lesko in the back row behind Richard Simmons, and he will be posed like he is trying to flick the back of Richard's ear. Richard will be crying, so I will have to somehow treat the hardboiled eggs in a special way to look more like crying eyes.

And then of course Bea Arthur will be there with a disapproving look on her face like my mom had when I caught pinworms in 10th grade. The doctor thought maybe they jumped out of an old baseball glove I found. Anyway, things are better now.

Bye,

Randy, your patient

Dr. Anderson,

Trust me, I've been trying to look back and find out why I feel this way. Every time I get past a certain point in my memory it all turns into that weird view of life where it's just like snapshots instead of movies. Also the problem with trying to remember details of long ago is that my mom always inserts her versions of these snapshots in the story. It's almost like she took my pictures and cut out some of the heads and replaced them with others. Like she always takes out her own face from the pictures of her doing anything like spanking me and replaces it with a picture of a cloud or a tree or some other landscape component. She doesn't remember any of these things.

And these pictures are in my head not hers, but she still changes them. Does that make sense? Is this weird that she can edit my memory or do I just trust her memory to fill in some of the other stuff I don't remember really well like the time my uncle Andy drew eye shadow on me with magic marker the day before school pictures? I looked really sleepy in that class picture.

My mom by the way is back playing the organ all the time and she now always flips the switch that makes it sound like a zither. That's okay for barn music but not on her latest craze that which consists of every Bobby Goldsboro song he ever sang. I'm going to eat now. The wiener soup is ready.

Bye,
Randy

Dr. Anderson,

Please send this to Mabel the bus driver. I bet you have friends who live around there where she might still be and they can deliver it or tell you the address. Thanks, Randy.

Dear Mabel,

I don't know if you're still alive or not but I remember you were the bus driver we had almost all the way through school. If you are not still alive I am sorry I didn't tell you sooner that I really appreciated the way you did your job although it is hard for someone in 6th grade generally to express how they feel about someone they take for granted.

So maybe now in life I know I took you for granted. I remember how you did anything you had to so that the bus would get us to school on time. I remember the sticky bandage from the first aid kit that you used to make the windshield wiper hold together that time. I remember too how the bus sometimes felt like the wheels were still very Mesolithic and the guys who carved them still hadn't figured out how to smooth it out just right. But I've been to tire factories and they don't carve them out of stone or rubber, they mix up all this goo and form it in a mold and then some guys might pick off all the stray parts that don't belong on a tire even if you buy it at Sears. It's similar to making lunchmeat only they wear gloves.

One time we had a big inner tube from a tire that was too big for your bus and you could get about four people on it in the lake before it tipped over and one guy named Brian got the inflator nozzle stuck on his swim trunks and he had to decide whether to get naked or drown. When he ran up on the beach you could tell which choice he made. It was always called "Brian's Naked Summer Adventure." Three girls saw him and I think an old lady too along with her husband who was either sleeping or dead because he didn't move all afternoon.

Also, I just want you to know that if you ever found a lunch bag on the bus that had a peanut butter and banana sandwich in it I don't like peanut butter and banana sandwiches and I thought it would be better to leave it on the bus rather than throw it out the window. A car could slip on it and hit a bridge or the sandwich could get caught in the wheel well and start to rot or worse yet attract a cat or a hungry beaver that would then get caught in the wheel and it would start a bad cycle of ruin. Besides, it would smell.

Also you should know that many lunches I had been actually looking forward to never made it to the school lunchroom or my stomach since there were these kids that would grab my lunch bag on the way to the lunchroom when I was in 8th grade. Sometimes I would get to the lunchroom and sit down to eat and I would then notice that my sandwich had a thumb hole in it. That's not too gross except the thumb probably wasn't too clean when it went into the sandwich. The kid who did it might have just come from art class or something where they worked with clay and I don't like the taste of clay much ever since that weird restaurant we at at in Iowa when I was 11.

Sometimes the kid would take my lunch out of my hand by grabbing it really fast and then I could barely keep it in sight as it got kicked down the hallway by about a thousand kids going to class or lunch. One time I found my lunch in the stairwell that goes up to where history and English were. It was mostly on the wall like bologna graffiti.

Anyway, please know your driving skills helped me get this far in life.

Thanks,
Randy Scuffle
(now in Chicago and not where you are)

Dr. Anderson,

Can you get me some buckets? Also the wiener truck didn't come this week. The reason I haven't been sleeping is because of the night flyers. They came back about a week ago. The blue ones this time, about twelve of them. They were beautiful and fast. I think it's a new model since the last time. They have such a great shine you can see the stars in them, which were really bright last night for the first time since all the rain. Maybe summer is finally here and I sure can't wait. This summer I just might take them up on their offer.

By the way, if you see anything about a bologna baby found on the Ravenswood tracks near Paulina, don't worry. I couldn't believe all the helicopters and lights!

Randy Scuffle

Silent blue aircraft
Reflective emissaries;
Bologna child born

Dr. Anderson,

Thanks again for letting me send you everything through e-mail. I dragged a lot of cables through the yard from the plug in the garage and I had to get three extension cords but it worked with the thick orange ones. I had to tape up all the rain gutter but it's sealed pretty well now and the cables in the rain don't worry me as much as before when every time I turned on the computer I'd cross my fingers that nothing would pop or spark and start the tent on fire. So even with all the rain I think it's pretty safe now.

My mom is back in the hospital again for her leg but also the ringing in her ears and now I can't figure out where I'm going to get some more buckets from. Already three are filled and the other two are starting to weigh more than before. You wanted to know how the job search was going and one thing my mom said before the accident with the wiener was that she would bring me more resume paper on the way home.

I like Office Depot™ paper. They have signs up in the store that say they don't hire people who are on drugs, so I know that their employees are happy to be there not because of drugs. When they smile they mean it. Also their lips don't click when they talk. That's a sign for sure that someone is stoned or on drugs to make you happy.

I saw on the commercials for drugs that the Claritin™ one makes you see the world in super 3D and all the people and clouds float around like they are cut out of cardboard and part of the background in a play like the one I was in back in fifth grade at St. Therese school. In that one, I noticed that all the trees and things only had colors like blue and green and yellow from the poster paints. I still can't smell that paint without thinking about the set-designing accident, and how the doctors kept laughing at me even after they got the brush out. By the way, I will look for more work soon but I can't think about just it yet. I will soon though,

Randy Scuffle

Dr. Anderson,

After all this time I still can't believe no one thought of putting a gate in the fence around the yard. My mom must have bought it from one of those fence places that advertise during the Saturday afternoon movie on the weird channels. You know how they can all put in a great fence or a porch and the pictures that they show in the ads look exactly like my memories of when I would visit my aunt and uncle when we were kids and the yard seemed so big and empty but that is because I was so little and everything seemed so big?

It just seems like a long time ago now, like the commercials for the junk yards that show a guy with a foot-wide watchband accepting $50 for his 1971 Chevy™ that's getting towed away. And you know by looking at the guy that he isn't an actor and the money they just handed him is going to supply his headband and fringed vest needs for about a month. He kind of reminds me of my uncle Andy.

While the people who built the fence are responsible for not putting in the gate, I don't think they are responsible for all the birds that sit on top of it. I never thought a bird could repaint a fence so fast, at least not the top four feet of it. Anyway, I have to go downtown tomorrow to do some stuff, so I have to finish the shovel bread now. Otherwise I'll be late.

Randy
Your patient

Dr. Anderson,

You should probably be aware of the fact that my mom hasn't stopped staring at me out her window for the last day or so, and even when I threw a snowball up at the window she didn't move much. I think she can see something over the back fence that is disturbing. I can't tell what it is since I am not that tall, but I will let you know after I come back from downtown. I'm really glad it's raining today though because it means spring is here and my shovel will be clean by the time I get back.

Randy

P.S. Will you please tell the meat truck to start parking in the alley??

> Promo at drive-in:
> Wiener and bun are dancing;
> Wiener jumps inside

Dr. Anderson,

I looked all over on the Internet and I can't find a replacement set of clown pants since I ripped the knee out on that rock. You'd think there would be a store that sold them. I've had these for a long time and even with all the mud they held up through winter. Do you think you could find a new source? I felt pretty embarrassed when someone gave me money downtown that I didn't even ask for. It's not like I'm poor or anything. I just had ripped pants. I will look one more time and if I find something I'll let you know so don't go too far out of your way shopping or going to the mall for this. Not yet anyway.

Randy

This is what I think a nest of baby terra-dogs might look like. Don't pay attention to them being in a tree. Baby wieners can't climb trees, at least not until they develop claws. Mostly I wanted to see if they'd look comfortable.

Dr. Anderson,

Please wait a while on the clown pants thing please. I found a place after all that has what I want but they are in Minnesota so I have to order through the mail. Just when I thought there was no place that had them, it turns out they have clown pants, shirts, tuxedoes, and even "clown style underwear," but I don't know what they look like because they weren't a pictured item.

I have always wondered why men's clothes always cost less than women's clothes and you'll never believe that the same problem exists in the world of clowns. The men's clown suits are about $200 but the women's clown suits are about $300 to $350. They both cover the same amount of body and they are both made with bright attractive colors and they are both probably also made of the same material. So why then is the women's clown suit more than the man's? It's a weird kind of discrimination.

I can't believe that the women's clown suit is made by a better designer. It sure didn't say it was a Christian Dior™ clown suit. Even if Christian Dior™ started making clown suits I doubt that they would be made to look just like everyone else's designs. And these weren't anything special. When I got my suit at the resale shop I only paid about $5 for it and that was in 2004! The worst thing mine ever did was bunch up really bad in the back where it also became discolored (probably from that time I sat on the paint.) Still, I'm really glad it was a cold weather clown suit, especially since my project to live in the yard started. This has been a cold spring and I am glad the birds are back even though the fence is creating lots of big shadows.

Anyway, the main reason I am writing is because I think I will order one of the new pant sets, but I also noticed I need one more bucket and a blanket for a special project I'm going to do. I want to make a bologna homeless person and see who will put money in his cup.

Thank you, and could you please remember to tell my mom to stop staring? Just call her or something, I'm sure she's hungry too.

Randy

Dear Mom,

I can't tell what you're staring at. There is nothing outside the yard except for the Baumgardners' dog Max and he is just tied up to a post by their back porch. I know you have to stop staring to get this message but when you do get it I want you to know I was trying to get you to stop. I will throw a mudball to make sure you are not dead and make sure it has no rocks in it. When you are done staring, if you can, please play that song I like from when we went to Disney World™ and rode on the little boats where there are about 1,000 little dolls from around the world singing. I can't remember the name of it though. It gets in my head almost as much as the theme song from this show I see in reruns called *Full House* which is also about little dolls but they don't live in a boat. They live on land in a house that is also lived in by Bob Saget, the guy who also used to be on that video show I used to watch. I liked the kids on that *Full House* show mainly because I can't ever tell if they are real or not and if they are not real, I really can't see the strings that make them work. TV is magic sometimes. Others on TV say those doll-girls are real and as older dolls they now have a line of products including clothes and perfumes. I wonder if they make clown pants.

Also, you should be aware of the fact that I took care of the gate problem in the fence and I will move the dirt to a better place tomorrow.

Oh, one more thing. Bob Saget might be the kind of person who would like to benefit from eternal Sea Monkey™ benefits.

Your son,
Randy

Dr. Anderson,

When I was downtown yesterday I saw a whole bunch of things that you would find interesting. I saw a guy who didn't have any arms and it hit me that he probably got pushed around a lot in school. I remember when I was in school the other kids really picked on the ones who were different. Like that time we had to play kill-ball in gym class because it was raining and we couldn't go out, so they saved the most goofy guy for last and then there was about 20 guys whipping balls at this guy who was kind of rubbery in a way so instead of just letting one of the balls hit him so the game would be over, he kept bending and avoiding the balls which kept smashing into the bleachers all folded up behind him.

And then the gym teacher let the guys throwing the balls get closer to try to end the game and they are about 10 feet away just smashing balls at this guy who everyone made fun of because he was a farmer. But he kept bending and jumping around like a garden gnome trying to dance to the beat of a car crushing machine.

The guy I saw yesterday though, who had no arms, he would have an advantage in that he had two fewer parts to hit. But on the other hand, he couldn't catch the balls either, and that is one of the ways you can make the guy throwing the ball have to leave the game. If you catch it, they're out. But he couldn't catch the balls because he didn't have any arms. Knowing how kids are in school, they would have aimed at his head probably, unless not having arms is a reason to get out of gym class.

When I was in school, they had a whole list of things that would get you out of gym class, and I don't remember not having arms being on the list. I still had to take gym class even after the accident with the carbon dioxide cartridge and the nail.

Randy

Dr. Anderson,

I realized today that I am still troubled by the whole clown pants thing for two reasons. First, and probably most important because it affects more people than just me, is that why are women's clown pants more expensive by about a third than men's clown pants? I think this is wrong and it has been in my head a lot like the times when I get songs in there that won't go away. But I don't want you to get this in your head either or you will be fixated and get a headache, like when I get the theme song from *Facts of Life* and it makes me crazy since I never watch it beyond the opening credits.

So remember I mentioned the aqua-dogs and the terra-dogs? Well I woke up the other morning and thought a nice complement to them would be flying aero-dogs. Each kind of living hot dog would have to have a job to do. Aqua-dogs are of course eager to help with the world food supply, but they would also be a great source of entertainment if you could swim with them instead of dolphins, which take up more space and shouldn't be on a menu. Terra-dogs would be happy to help with the food problem too, but in the meantime, they could cut the grass or help children cross the street. Aero-dogs might be useful to help deliver letters to members of Congress, who could be walking across Washington, get a polite tap on their shoulder from an aero-dog, which then delivers a timely message of support just before a special Congressional hearing. It would also remind Congress to think up more recipes for the *Congressional Hot Dog Cook Book*, which has been sadly out of print for some time now. I am, however, fortunate to own a copy!

Thanks, Dr. Anderson,
Randy

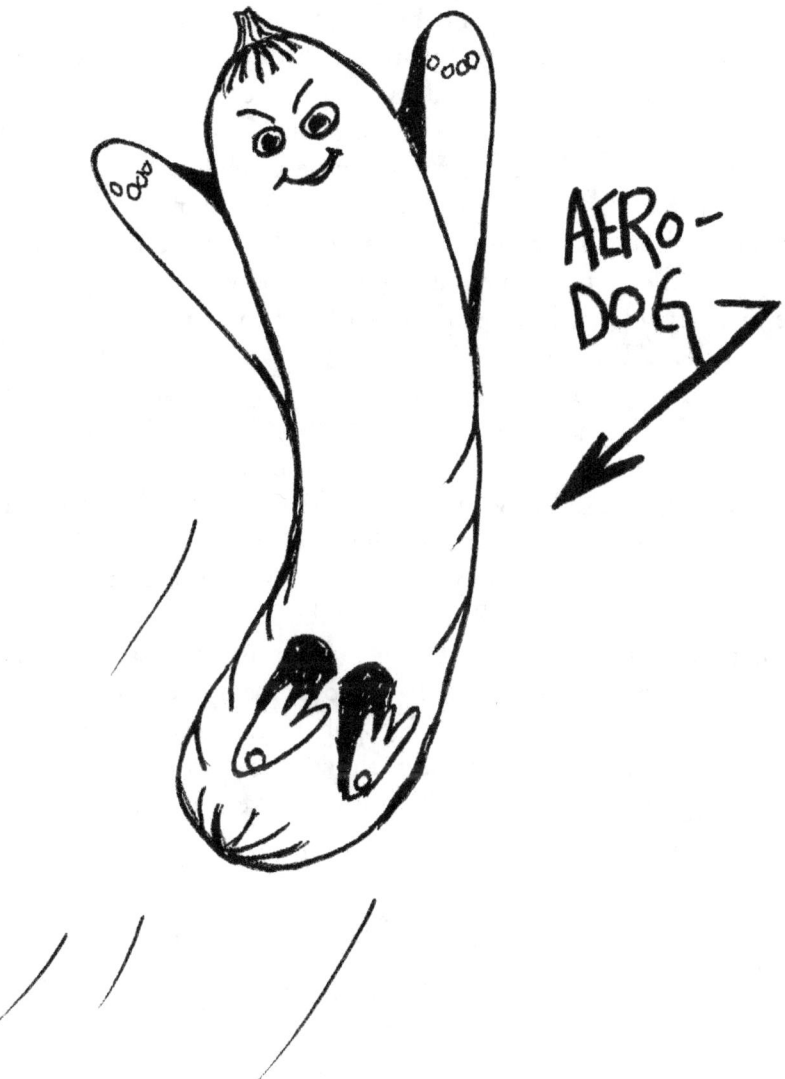

AERO-
DOG

Dr. Anderson,

I was thinking the other day a lot about two things. One, the idea that gravity is just God's way of keeping humans from messing up the rest of the universe. It's like glue or more likely like being a dog with a chain around its neck so that it doesn't crap in the next door neighbor's yard like used to happen when the Boofer family lived across the alley from us. I would argue that humans are pretty messy, but we oddly think other animals are dirty. So if there is a God, he probably didn't want us contaminating the rest of the universe with our junky old cars, used baby diapers and muskrat heads nailed to boards.

I saw once, at a barn that sold antiques in Wisconsin, many different animal heads nailed to boards shaped like the plaques you would get for selling a lot of candy during your money raising event to send the high school band to Oakland or Miami to compete in marching competitions. They would get big trophies if they win but they get a plaque (without the animal head) if you lose. The stupid thing was that they had animals you don't even have to hunt in order to get their heads off. There was a rat head on one board with two mouse heads also on it. And it was spray-painted gold. Also they had a deer and a goat and a beaver or something. I couldn't tell because I don't remember if beavers are supposed to be cross-eyed or that's just those big pond rats they have in Pennsylvania during Cretaceous periods.

So anyway, I think God is trying to keep us from leaving six-pack rings on other planets because it would probably be sad to see alien ducks strangled to death by foreign polymers. Oh, and I almost forgot - the other thing I have been thinking about a lot lately is the song "Sugar Sugar" by the Archies. I don't like it or anything, it just won't get out of my head.

Bye,
Randy

Dr. Anderson,

The fence has a bunch of holes in it thanks to weather changes and now there are eyes that keep looking at me through them. All I see is the eye but I am pretty sure it's in someone's head. This has been going on for about a week, and I'm starting to wonder what all the excitement is about. Maybe you can see some kind of Madonna (the real Madonna, not Madonna™) or Jesus image on one of our windows when you look through the hole just right. Wouldn't that be interesting to find out my mom's bedroom window had a holy apparition on it? All I see is a bunch of smears, and I'm pretty sure one of them is from that bird I heard hit the window the other day.

That made me wonder too about the idea that human death is just the same as when a bird flies into a window. What if there is a pane of glass with everyone's name on it? Of course you couldn't see your name on it because you could then walk around the one with your name on it. It would be kind of funny too if God saw the whole episode as if you were walking into a pane of glass being carried by a couple of comedy glass installation experts. Then, if it wasn't your time to die, the glass installation experts would be walking back and forth trying to avoid you but you're kind of ignorant about the whole thing and you keep veering toward the glass. Actually, if you hit the glass even though they tried to avoid you, it would be the same as a suicide. Anyway, I don't know if there is a God (the real God, not God™) so these images in the window might be grease. Can you send another box of microscope slides?

Thank you,

Randy, your patient

Dr. Anderson,

I almost forgot to tell you about the summer I decided to go to Bible school but had second thoughts about the whole thing when it occurred to me that there might be a street preaching class. The thought of doing a directed study that consisted of nothing more than standing on a corner with a microphone talking about Jesus and homosexuals stunned me into a whole new level of doubt.

Can there be levels of agnosticism, Dr. Anderson? Maybe it's all or nothing, and there are no levels. If you are an agnostic that means you can't really make up your mind about it, so really you have no opinion and you might as well be an atheist. I just figure that something like this you can't really be on the fence about. I like the way my mom always said "if there was a God he must have wanted me to suffer." So she pretty much suffers whether there is a God or not. It's her decision, just as it's her decision to not clean up all the palm prints on the new big window in her bedroom. Now she has a panoramic view by the way.

I knew the construction guys were lying when they said they'd be back to clean up all the nails and insulation that fell into the yard. My mom probably has no idea that they didn't even put the siding back on around the window. It's not even that hard to do. I saw Dean Johnson do it on *Hometime* on Saturday morning where he fixes up houses and shows you how to do your own siding and stuff. The weird thing is that in the background you always see his wife digging a hole or cutting a hole in a wall.

Once you've read a book about being buried alive you can't watch that show without wondering how innocently she is unwittingly digging her own grave on live TV. Trust me on this one, there are about five women who have been on that show, and only JoAnne Liebeler has managed to dig her way out. You never see the other ones again. Ever. Also, if you could send another network card for my Linux machine that would be great since the butter knife broke off at a weird angle and I can't ping myself.

Thank you, Randy

Dr. Anderson,

Yesterday I was watching a squirrel taunt a dog and it dawned on me that matter at our scale might behave the same way it does on an atomic or subatomic scale. So if you smash a neutron into an electron or a proton, it breaks apart and for a really small amount of time there are other types of particles. It made me wonder if you smash bologna hunks together, do you see similar types of particles or hunks always produced after the collision? I need a camera to try this out, preferably video with color and slow motion. Also, I'm almost out of compressed nitrogen. Please send more!

Thank you,

Randy Scuffle Jr . (if I had a twin which of us would be junior, Dr. Anderson?)

Dr. Anderson,

The most exciting thing happened. I remembered I knew this girl who swore she used to work at a bologna factory. I can't believe I forgot all about this. I don't know where she is now but she says bologna starts out as a pink slurry in a big vat. Then she said it is poured into molds and then it naturally cures into the familiar shapes we usually see bologna in before it gets processed and turned into energy for your day of activities.

I especially like to eat a lot of bologna before I go to museums like the Art Institute of Chicago. They have all these treasures of the world upstairs, and downstairs they have restaurants that might serve hot dogs or something but I'm pretty sure I saw a sign that says they were about $10 each. This I think is a great statement in support of my hot-dog and bologna art project. Already there is a connection at a famous art museum between bologna and art.

So, I was thinking that if the bologna people at Oscar Mayer™ took special orders maybe I could draw up a design for a bologna statue or something and they could pour it into my mold. I could even make the mold too, but I would certainly have to find something other than my buckets for the molds, otherwise the statues would all have bucket-shaped heads and hands and feet. Probably the torsos would be bucket-like too. A bucket would be a good mold only if you wanted to make bologna buckets. A cool idea maybe at first until you realize the handles would probably shrivel up and crack before the show opened.

But if I figured out how to make the molds they could fill them, I then could finish my "Holy Bologna Family™" piece which would be the hit of the new art season on Navy Pier. (That's where any art that's better than the art sold at suburban hotels is found.) Maybe if I treat it using the soon-to-be-patented Bolognafication™ process, it would last until the Christmas season; then it could be in the window of the former Marshall Fields™, which is now Macy's™, or even on the street.

And on top of that, people would be hungry from riding the Ferris wheel and having their pictures taken with people in dog suits (or something). I'm not sure what the official Chicago animal is. It might be the dog. I never heard the mayor say anything about dogs though, so it could be some kind of a fish or maybe an animal we never see around anymore since the city got so big. I saw a bunch of opossums under the neighbor's porch a year ago. Maybe that's why they moved away so quickly. I would nominate the terra-dog if I could.

Anyway, if the people are hungry, maybe we could create a bologna-*art* version of the statue and a bologna-*food* version of the statue. Then people could take a bite out of the baby Jesus if they wanted to pay US $10 and get a t-shirt that says "I bit baby Jesus™ and I love bologna" or something. Let me know if you want to get in on this so I can start designing the brochures. I've got to go now, my mom is kissing the window again.

Randall Scuffle
Chicago

> Raccoons, squirrels, rats;
> Marsupials under porch;
> Coveting hot dogs

Dr. Anderson,

This is going to be a distressing week for me what with the loss of the latest batch of Sea Monkeys™ and the fact that as of today, Ryan Seacrest™ has still not answered my offer to help him live forever. I figure he is probably busy with his radio show and his television shows and I think he now has a line of clothing, which I never thought he would do because I didn't know that radio people were also good clothing designers. I'd wear his clown pants if he made them, but Ryan Seacrest™ probably doesn't design or even like clown pants. I figure that because he spent so much of his time hanging around teenagers and the latest music he didn't really have the time to go shopping for something new that would completely change the way he sits.

I am so happy I found out the benefits, especially in the winter, when the wind whips through everything, of thermal clown pants. They are hard to find. Believe me. Not that many people appreciate them. They hold in the heat, you know. Sometimes that's bad.

Anyhow, I figured the Sea Monkeys™ died because of an imbalance of something, probably some electrolytes were not in the proper proportion. Which reminds me, can you send new eye droppers and a different mug? The one I currently use has a chip and my lip gets raw.

Just so you know, my mom says you are building a case against me and that she will soon have her revenge. I can't figure out why that would be since she is the one with the webbed toes, not me. Besides, you are here to help. One last thing, please let me know if you still know that guy who used to work with Jason Alexander™, as I'd like to get his address and ask him about my monkey movie theory. I say it's real.

Randy Scuffle, your patient in Chicago...

Dr. Anderson,

I recently ran out of Popscicle™ sticks that are a mandatory part of my backyard laboratory. I use them to make my own cutting boards for the meat experiments and testing sequences. They stay together pretty well if you use the right glue but I discovered for sure that you don't want to use the kind they use to stick hardhats to steel beams because if you inhale too much of it you end up building a model of what looks like a two-story outhouse.

Even though most outhouses don't have windows, the one I made did, and I am sure I started out making a meat-cutting plank. Also, there wasn't much glue left and it became apparent that clown pants stick pretty well after they melt from the glue. Anyhow, some parts of the pants are still stuck to the picnic table except for the pieces that are now in squirrel nests. So if you could please sent a couple of cases of them (I think they are sold where Brownies and Cub Scouts go for projects) that would be great.

Also, I should alert you that an impostor has been influenced by my earlier art projects, specifically the bologna baby doorstep surprise. My art is free to be enjoyed. There is no delivery fee or ransom. If you find a bologna baby in a basket on your doorstep it is yours forever. That's wrong to make people pay to be the brunt of your artwork. Art should not have a brunt. I believe it has a hull, but not a brunt.

Your patient, Randy Scuffle

> Aero-dog angels
> Whisper in ears of Congress:
> "Sea Monkeys™ can help"

Dr. Anderson,

Would you please send this letter to your friend at the post office in Washington? I think that's where the head guy is and maybe he will listen to this idea if it comes from a friend.

Dear Post Office,

I know you are having lots of trouble with money and also with trying to fit the magazines through our front door because they come all shredded and sometimes they are bent even when it says "do not bend." The other day we got a magazine that was all crumpled up and it had no back cover and it had donut stains on it or maybe they were from some kind of dripping fish sandwich or even a bunch of hot wings. I'm pretty sure it was *not* salad dressing.

So anyway, I was thinking that my mom always puts all my mail in this box before shoving it down the slide and the box of junk is getting heavier and heavier because there is always more and more to put in. So I was thinking about this idea that would save the Post Office a lot of money and at the same time would probably help keep the spines of your workers from twisting up like knots before blowing out and ruining their shirts in the process. Here is my idea:

Instead of giving the people who send lots of junk through the mail the discounted postal rates, why not give the people who send hardly anything through the mail a lower stamp rate? Then you can charge extra for the people who clog up your system with all kinds of promotions for stuff I never need. Probably there will be a bunch of them who say "forget it" and don't send out all the junky advertising for barbells and toenail creams, leaving your postal carrier's bags lighter. This will also help with efficiency because there will be less junk to sort through. I never heard of you delivering junk mail 40 years late but I have heard of you delivering love letters and post cards 40 years late because it got lost behind a cabinet or something.

So if I want to mail a letter to my mom it should cost a dime, but if someone wants to try to sell me a rubberized lawn protector, they have to pay 62 cents or 73 cents. I think that would be great. Also, I think too that your workers will be less inclined to shove stuff through the door-hole even though it would never fit. I once got a magazine that had a scratch on it and they put it in a separate bag and enclosed an apology for ruining it. But the donut mail recently didn't have a bag or an apology. It still had sugar on it too.

By the way, I still have all the buckets and boxes of mail my mom slid into the yard, and I should probably go through it. Is it legal to make an art project from unopened mail?

Thank you,

Randy Scuffle, Chicago

P.S. My uncle worked at the Post Office for a while but he had to quit because he said it felt like he worked underwater. Not that it made him all pruny or anything but that he couldn't understand what anyone said and everything moved so slowly, like when he had that stroke.

> Girls in magazines
> Smell like the perfume inserts;
> And they always stare

Dr. Anderson,

I am sorry I have not written for a while, and I know you must be worried that I am not working on my problems, but I want you to know I have been working on some other things and it has been educational. For one thing, I never heard from Ryan Seacrest™ about wanting to live forever, which I can help him do with the help of course of the Sea Monkeys™ that have been specially trained.

It's probably a good thing Ryan has not responded just yet because I figured out that in order to train the Sea Monkeys™ to eat a person's brain plaque, I have to have a little bit of that person to use as a training incentive. Or at least get them used to the flavor. I don't know if it matters what Ryan tastes like to the Sea Monkeys™ or not, but if I can get them wanting more of his flavor, especially before they are released inside to do their life-giving job, then it will be more successful. I suppose it would be best to get some of his brain plaque but I doubt he would want to send a sample through the mail, what with all the boxes that get kicked around and lost and then you know sometime in the future or about 50 years, they will find this brain plaque sample at a post office or a UPS™ warehouse and try to deliver it to me. That's probably not a good idea because I might be in the bomb shelter and miss their visit.

Anyhow, Ryan Seacrest™ might want to know that I have discovered this way to ensure success, and then he will be more likely to share a sample. Right now I am only offering this to Ryan Seacrest™ and maybe Regis Philbin, Barbara Walters and Joan Rivers, as I would be afraid to see someone like Paris Hilton™ live forever, or worse yet those Kardashian™ people. I have standards, and I wouldn't want to be responsible for that and no matter how good the bomb shelter is, people might find me and express their frustration. Besides, I think Paris might taste like that perfume that always makes me sneeze because it reminds me of bug spray. I accidentally got some near one of the Sea Monkey™ buckets last summer and they all clumped up.

Randy Scuffle, your patient

Dr. Anderson,

I think probably the best way to get a sample from Ryan Seacrest™ is to get an old Kleenex™ that he has blown his nose into, and there should be enough of him in there for the Sea Monkeys™ to sample and begin to enjoy his flavor. I think this is the best approach because I noticed that they don't do so well with anything chunky. Once these are trained, they should pass along their taste preferences to their off-spring, who should then be naturally ready to eat his brain plaque so he can live forever.

I noticed the other night he was not at the top of his game, and it may be an early sign that he is starting to deteriorate mentally, which could mean he is ready for his own family of brain plaque-eating Sea Monkeys™. I would really like to get them to him while he is still young, but you never know how old people in Hollywood really are since they have makeup and they drink from straws all the time so they naturally pucker for pictures. Anyhow, if you would please let me know if you know anyone who has access to some Ryan Seacrest™ head-goo, have them send it to me in a plastic bag. I will start train-ing them immediately. It probably wouldn't be a bad idea to resubmit my request to him and just ask for a sample either just to be safe.

Randy Scuffle, your patient

Dr. Anderson,

I was inspired recently by something that gave me an idea for an artistic statement. This one is not quite like the bologna babies project I once did which worked quite well but I understand caused some problems for a neighbor who found one of them. This involves setting up a little stage like a puppet theatre but instead of puppets I would put some of the meat sculptures I do of the latest presidential candidates in there. Of course, if one of the candidates wants to be represented in something like olive loaf I would do that too since I have connections for big quantities. The pepper loaf doesn't work so well unless you leave the pepper on as hair but that only works if the person you are sculpting in meat has hair that looks like pepper loaf.

Anyway, the two candidates would just sit in the puppet stage and there would be a voice track playing random sentences as if they were debating but not really listening to each other. The spooky thing about debates is that in today's debates, the debater doesn't engage with the other debater. The debater is really talking to the audience, even though the debater is looking at the opponent. In order to really make it real, there should be another voice track that represents the audience's thoughts, like "he looks good in olive loaf" or "she should be wearing pepper" or something like that.

Mostly you know I've been concentrating for a while on heads, so these wouldn't be life-size like the ones I wanted to do for the class reunion. Boy, that didn't work out very well, especially since that one guy from high school thought they were appetizers. I also thought it might be kind of fun to get rid of my oversupply of hot dogs and bind some of them together to form carving blocks, but then someone would accuse me of trying to be Picasso. And I'm not.

I'm Randy Scuffle, your patient. Bye.

Dr. Anderson,

I couldn't figure out where the break in the Internet line was, and just couldn't get connected. It took most of the week to figure it out and it turns out the squirrels did it again. They apparently buried a nut next to the one spot I didn't have the cable covered with that rubber hose I found in the yard next door when our neighbors threw it away. I figured it would work to protect the cable but of course the squirrels around here like to play tricks on me when I don't find them enough nuts. They have become lazy and I can spend hours just finding them nuts and by the time they are full I don't have a whole lot of time to mix up some wiener soup. I figure once all the rain and snow stops they will find more of their own food, but I think I have meanwhile proven one side effect of living like a squirrel: they take advantage of your good will. So if you could do me a favor and send a bag of dried corn cobs that would be great, especially if they still have corn on them. I'm going to leave those out but make them work for it. So anyway that's why it took so long to write this week.

Also, corn reminds me of this show on TV where they used to build a new house for people who have a tragedy and have been living in shacks. You can't really make fun of the people on the show because they all have diseases and tragedy or have to go to the bathroom in plastic bags hanging over a hole, but you can find a lot of corn flowing, especially the creamy kind, when that loud guy screams everything.

He reminds me of that guy in the question mark suit who claims to be Matthew Lesko™ and sells you books on how to get the government to enrich your life. The new house show used to be more interesting when they showed how they build the houses and they had stress doing it in a week but then it changed and became a formula. I would like to see the show come back to re-visit some of the people they built houses for to see if they kept them clean or if they have turned into dumps or if the neighbors hate them because they got a house and whether or not the IRS™ stopped by to assess what they might be able to get out of the deal. I have not heard any stories about it though.

If we were on that show and got sent to Disney World™ for a vacation I would be bored unless there was a way to celebrate without hearing that song they always play at weddings called "Celebrate." I think they also play it at sports events, parties, and use it to promote car salesmanship.

Remember the Toyota™ Sellathons? And how they used to make you feel you had to buy a car to help them reach *their* sales goal and if they did *you* could feel like you were part of the success? I think that is what America should be all about. When companies make a lot of money, we should get a badge or something. Maybe a medal or a magnetic ribbon to put on the car that says "I did my part to support corporate profits."

Anyhow, if you could send the corn that would be great, and I forgot one other thing: I still have not heard from any of the governors on the statue proposal. And I can't wait till this presidential thing is done so I can get to work on whoever is going to be the candidate. This is taking so long my meat is getting dry.

Randy Scuffle, your patient

Black pitted olives,
Green olives with pimentos,
Taxidermy eyes

Dr. Anderson,

I remember you knew someone who worked on television. Do you think you could forward this letter to them so they could get it to Ryan Seacrest™? Thanks.

Mr. Ryan Seacrest™,

As noted in my previous communications, I am Randy Scuffle, an artist living in Chicago and I work in various mediums including, but not limited to, meat. I also have ideas that I would like to share and if you want to hear them great, but if not that's okay too, but I mainly want to know if you'd be interested in a project I'm working on that has two prongs. By the way, I always thought your name sounded like the name of an aftershave or maybe a piece of driftwood that was all smooth. It's just very soothing. Anyway, here are the two prongs:

First, I read somewhere that you want to have a long career, which is great. I am developing a breed of Sea Monkey™ that is small enough to live inside of heads like yours, and I am developing them to have a taste for brain plaque. So the idea is that if you have a colony of Sea Monkeys™ in your head and they feed off of your brain plaque as it develops you will probably never get old and you will also have the memory of a young person but not so young that you are like a chimp. Let me know if you are interested. Your plan to be the new Dick Clark could be enhanced by this idea.

Second, and I make this offer only to the most interesting people, I would like you carve your head out of bologna. You also have a choice of olive loaf. You, as the object have a choice in how you are portrayed. Bologna or olive loaf. I assure you I only use the finest raw materials and I have also perfected a soon-to-be-patented Bolognafication™ process that keeps the meat from getting full of worms or flies, which would not be good, especially once the inside where your brain would be gets hollowed out and infested. I respect my art-form and I make sure everything is made to the highest level of quality. That means no flies in your brain. Let me know if you are interested, as I know you are busy with all your jobs. Also, consider what kind of olives you want me to use for your eyes. I can't tell if you are a plain Spanish (no pimentos!) or something more ruddy.

Also, in order for me to start training the customized Sea Monkeys™, they need some kind of starter flavoring. This will help them acclimate to only your brain plaque. I think the best thing you could send me would be a used Kleenex™ or perhaps some earwax on a stick. From this, I would train the Sea Monkeys™ to enjoy cleaning out your brain so you can not only think clearly, but to do so forever. Please put these in a zipper type plastic bag but not the kind with the double zippers because those are a pain and the drippings get caught in between the zippers and it makes a mess, no matter what they say on the commercials.

Thank you,

Randy Scuffle (this was probably forwarded from a friend of yours from Dr. Anderson, who knows all about me.)

> Recipe for soup:
> Boil water, add the hot dogs
> Boil more, don't burn lips

Dr. Anderson,

I have always wondered if when you go to Hollywood they make you sign a contract that guarantees you will have some degree of fame, but in the contract there is a clause that says you will have to make a movie with a monkey. You can choose either to do it early in your career or put it off until later in your career, but you will *have* to make a monkey movie or television episode. Clint Eastwood did it; Jason Alexander did it (did you ever get his address?); everyone from *Friends* did it; every sitcom ever made had an episode with a monkey in it; Charleton Heston did it in *Planet of the Apes*; everyone did it in *The Wizard of Oz;* Johnny Depp did it; Ronald Reagan did it and that's what makes me think about this: there is an inverse correlation between the degree of shame and the degree of fame. I will design a chart depicting this correlation and share it with you. I could probably think of more examples except I'm now getting hungry for a banana.

Which also reminds me: one time this guy I know said one of the funniest things in the world is a man in a tuxedo eating a banana. Which is true if you think about it. Maybe monkeys and apes rule the world.

Your patient,
Randy

Golden scepter waved,
Ryan Seacrest's™ monkeys kneel,
Benevolent King

Dr. Anderson,

I just wanted to update you on this song thing. I still get songs in my head, and sometimes it is a good song. But mostly, when I get songs in my head they are what I consider bad songs. They are the songs that I only know one part of and it goes around like a gerbil in one of those exercise wheels. Yesterday it was "Polly Wolly Doodle" which is not a song you hear much on the radio anymore, but somehow it got put in my brain. I think it might have been from watching old variety shows that featured the King family or the Osmonds or something because I am sure there was no television back when that song was written. Anyhow, it is pretty frightening to know that the guy on the bus with the sunglasses and the leather coat is probably listening to rap or death metal and I've got "Polly Wolly Doodle" in my head all day. The worst part is when the chorus turns into the Mormon Tabernacle Choir and I get that feeling like when you step off the curb unexpectedly.

So what has changed in America so much that you could never imagine Madonna™ singing "Polly Wolly Doodle" even though it is a traditional American song that people used to love? Dr. Anderson, if you still know that person who works at the record company this is probably a good idea, and I want to share it.

It would be great if Madonna™ could do a whole album of songs from around the campfire. She could dress like either a camper or a cowgirl, and sing her adaptations of these songs and I'm sure that, as usual, people would say she is so smart to think of it. I wouldn't even want credit for this, but it would be great if I could do a bologna sculpture of her for the cover, only I would make sure there wasn't a pimento stuck between her teeth. Probably I'd use pure bologna instead of olive loaf like I did for Richard Simmons, but you have to admit the radish sprouts made his hair look pretty real.

I have to go now. The squirrels are pretty hungry again.

Randy Scuffle (your patient)

Dr. Anderson,

Over the weekend I woke up and a bunch of squirrels were staring at me already waiting for breakfast. It turns out I forgot to change the clocks ahead an hour, but somehow they knew the time had changed. I tried to find some nuts for breakfast but since the grass is still all brown and wet from the snow melting I couldn't really feel much with fingernails full of mush and grass. This new experiment to live like a squirrel is going well otherwise, and is more satisfying than my pigeon experiment, which was okay until I realized no matter how hard I tried I could never really fly without a helicopter or jet. And considering the kind of places they have been building around here lately, I would imagine you could build a helicopter pad on top of one of them for size alone but I doubt that the cinder blocks would be strong enough to hold up a helicopter even though most of the time a helicopter is holding up itself. I don't mean that like a holdup because then you'd be pointing the gun at yourself and saying "this is a holdup" and that would be kind of dumb.

So anyway I was wondering why the squirrels have become so dependent on me to find their nuts after they were the ones that buried them. In the fall you can see the holes they dug to bury them but by spring you have to sniff around pretty much to find where they are. And they are better equipped for that than I am. I can smell pretty well even considering that boiling wiener soup sneeze last year, but I figure I am taller than a squirrel so it follows that they must be closer to the ground. I tried the sniffing thing and it works pretty well until my pants are cold and wet on the knees and then I just want to sit down but then the rest of my pants get cold and wet and the silk doesn't dry out real fast. Plus you can kind of see through it pretty much except where the blue and red dots are. Anyhow, I have to set the clocks ahead now and I can tell you I'm pretty happy with the sun being out for the first time. I think the squirrels are happy too and as a joke they stole some of the wiener tips I saved from the last batch of soup.

Randy Scuffle
Your patient

Dr. Anderson,

I have a new series of art pictures I will show you soon just for your enjoyment. It is part of the wiener series of art projects. Or hot dog. I don't know what I want to call it yet. It's like when you get a puppy and you don't know what to name it and after a year of calling him Spork you realize he is really more of a Norman, and then you don't want to change his name because its papers would need to be changed. Then, if it's a kid (and not a dog) they are almost ready for school and probably know their name already.

When I was in school there was a kid named Nippy and everyone called him Nippy and you know how there are kids with you in kindergarten, and then you lose track of them, but they show up in 5th grade again, and you realize you know each other? Well it turned out his name was Billy and he had a speech problem. I think that's how we lost track of each other because he was sent off to speech school and came back with a different name. Anyhow, I kind of liked him better when I thought his name was Nippy. So watch out for the pictures soon. Probably in a week or so.

Okay, this has been bothering me lately and I have to admit it. When we say we fight for our freedom isn't it kind of like when your kid is afraid to grow up and still wants to be irresponsible? Isn't the kid really just fighting to remain irresponsible? What if when we say "freedom" we really mean "irresponsibility," almost as if we are a nation of children? What if our whole country is really just 300 million 35-year-old guys who won't move out of their parents' houses?

I have to go now. A giant icicle formed on the garage and is hanging over where I let the shovel bread cool off. By the way, I thought I saw a beaver the other day but I realized it was this hat I thought I had lost before the snow started. Chicago winters can laugh at you that way.

Randy Scuffle

Dr. Anderson,

Today it is so cold I can't even pull the hot dogs off the nails, which is usually pretty easy because of their natural tendency to give off a little bit of grease from inside the hot dog meat. They are frozen solid. I just put them out last night so that the animal with the claws couldn't get to them anymore. I didn't know opossums, raccoons and wolverines ate hot dogs, but I guess when you are cold and hungry you'll eat almost anything. I don't mean that hot dogs are bad for you, it's just that I didn't think that animals would have evolved with hot dogs in their diet, unless hot dogs are among the oldest foods known, like nuts and Twinkies™. I'm pretty sure that when hot dogs were invented no one thought, "Hey, I wonder if animals will like these as a treat worth stealing from Randy." In fact I'm positive.

I had this dream this morning that you'd find interesting, Dr. Anderson. In it, I was on top of a telephone pole, and I could see all around, and it was like I had super-vision. I could see the relationships people had that they didn't even know, like for example I could see all the people who were thinking about getting a cup of coffee and they had little cups of coffee over their heads like in the old commercial with Cream of Wheat™ or in those commercials with the goofy guy eating Arby's™ roast beef sandwiches and he has a cartoon Arby's™ hat on his head. I think the hat looks a lot like something that you wouldn't want to leave on the bus for little kids to find, but I figure whoever does their marketing must know what they're doing otherwise it wouldn't have become a TV commercial.

Anyhow, the hot dogs are like hammers and I am hungry, so I can steam them off the nails if I hold the nail board over the hot water for a while. I think the presidential head sculpture out of meat project will keep me busy at least until spring, but I have to find another name for it that's artistic like "Buzzard Perch™" or something...I have to think about it...

Bye, Dr. Anderson,

Randy

P.S. I read in the paper that olives are on sale this week at Jewel™. If you could call them to make sure these are not the small ones, that would be great. They make the eyes look all beady, which may be okay for a bust of Ted Cruz but not for subjects with an inquisitive nature.

Thanks Dr. Anderson!

Randy

> Terra-dogs are fast
> Aqua-dogs swim, Aeros fly;
> Rock, Paper, Scissors

Dr. Anderson,

So guess what? Last night I had a dream that not only were the wheels stolen off the golf cart and then I had to walk home (which is weird because the golf cart battery died a long time ago), but I dreamed that I could see like a bug. Apparently, I had multiple eyes or some kind of bug eye that lets me see all around me and it was really weird but really kind of nice because I didn't have to turn my head around to look at things behind me.

It just takes a while to sort out where you are looking and what the front looks like and what the back looks like. The hard part about that is getting used to the fact that it can all be moving separately with different things going on, like this big television I saw once that had a bunch of different, smaller pictures going on at the same time. Like sportscasters no doubt. The other thing that was kind of hard to get used to was the blurry streaks everything left behind, especially if it had a lot of color or was attached to a running dog. Which reminds me of this guy in third grade who had a dog that would run around all the time and bark at everything and it never just sat there. It ran around the house until it had made a path in the grass, which was bad because there wasn't much grass to start with. Their yard was mostly pool, which his mom always sat near with a drink all summer.

I don't think she ruined the grass because it was mostly in a big circle, but you could tell where her chair had been, and the drinks. She also would wear some kind of dancing leotard or something, and sunglasses. I didn't really pay attention because I was only in third grade, but I could tell right away it wasn't at all like my mom, who was probably at home repairing accordions or telling my dad about how her hair had nerves in it. She never cut her hair even after the marshmallow incident.

Anyhow, I know I promised to update you on the wiener gun, but I've got to get the fire going before it gets dark.

Your patient,
Randy Scuffle

Dr. Anderson,

Okay I admit it probably wasn't the best thing in the world to try but at the time I thought it would work. Remember the frozen boot I told you about? Well, it didn't come unstuck even though it was really warm here for a couple of days. So I thought filling it with hot wiener soup would help it thaw out, and it should have worked, except I ended up trying to get the reindeer standing back up all afternoon since suddenly my mom wants to talk to me, and all she cares about is the lighted reindeer, and how it is on its side like it is dead, and she is starting to talk about omens.

My mom does this all the time and I can't believe she even knows how to ride a bus let alone drive, but that's probably a good thing based on all the information I gave you a long time ago about her driving and the accident and the wiener stuck in the wiper. That didn't end up like I thought it would and so even after the golf cart died, she now makes me go everywhere for everything. A carton of milk has a few omens in it if you ask her, but I don't believe in all that stuff, not since I realized that you can carve ham in the shape of anything you want, like a brain, for example. If all of our brains are just like ham, then someone with a knife or artist carving tools can pretty much make you think whatever they want. And for my money, there is nothing less interesting than having my thoughts carved out for me by someone with a vision of what my ideas should be. I will carve ham, but not if it belongs to someone else.

Anyhow, it got really cold again while I was making the reindeer stand up again, and now the boot is filled with frozen wiener soup and locked in a frozen puddle. Spring is just around the corner though, so I will wear extra socks until then.

Randy Scuffle
Your patient

Dr. Anderson,

Sometimes I see interesting things in my head when I close my eyes, especially after a big bowl of wiener soup...

My mom still has no idea the bomb shelter is here, but I guess her dad wanted it hidden real well so no one would break in and take all his napkins and beans, which there are plenty of, and for some reason about 2,000 packets of salt and sugar. If these interesting things I see represent what is in my mind, what do all the dark spots mean? I think I know, but have to go now...

Randy Scuffle
Your patient

> In my last nightmare,
> Clown shoes on telephone wires
> A very sad day

Dr. Anderson,

Okay it got pretty cold again and I was completely thrown off by the earlier warmer weather, which created not only puddles in the yard, but presented a challenge to keep all of the Sea Monkeys™ from totally freezing up into a block of ice. It could have been really bad like when my dad brought home all those smelts that time in the ice and they all looked kind of surprised that they had been frozen while swimming. But they were still good. Maybe that was the best thing and they had no idea what was going to happen. Now that I think about it though, I really try to avoid any food that can look surprised before it gets eaten. I think the last thing in your head before you get eaten shouldn't be "what?" as you realize you are about to get knocked off as part of some kind of farming operation. I believe they do this with fish and cows, as well as some other types of animals like hams.

Anyway, I don't think there are any farms on this planet yet for humans, at least not that I know of, but then again, if we were being farmed how would we even know we were being farmed? Do trout know their destiny? I think that is an interesting question to ask. I don't speak trout but my mom says a kid at her school was born with gills so he had to wear turtlenecks, which is a whole other animal.

So the reason I haven't written for a while is that the keyboard got frozen to the tarp and I know I shouldn't have left it there but it was really warm and then it got really cold and the thing got frozen. Meanwhile, I lost one of my boots in the slush again and it got frozen in too, and so I've been pretty much stuck in the shelter until now, when the temperature hit at least 50 the other day. It was weird because all the snow was melting and I kept telling myself that it's still cold enough to not ruin the blocks of bologna that I just had delivered for the big election year sculpture project.

I still plan, as I think I told you before, to carve out each of the major candidates according to my style which is unique in the art world. I plan, once we know who the major candidates will be, to sculpt them in bologna or, in the case of any candidate with a preference, I will use olive loaf. The only problem with that is the olives sometimes fall out and makes them look more pocked and incomplete than if it is solid, trustworthy bologna.

Anyhow, I am pretty sure I have perfected a lot of my talent over the past winter, since I didn't have much to do but tend the soup and then of course wait for the keyboard to get unstuck. It works pretty well I guess. Also, I will try to capture the most natural looks for the candidates, even if it includes anger or surprise. I will then offer it to them as an honored gift, which is only fitting since they need to know they touch our lives every day. The least I could do is carve out their heads in meat, which is my favorite medium.

Despite what my mother probably told you, I don't eat paste anymore, but every once in a while I like to open a fresh bottle of mucilage and it reminds me of my third grade teacher Mrs. Glending, who had soft hands. They weren't sticky like glue, just soft. Like olive loaf. Anyhow, I have to go now, the batteries are starting to blink for a charge, and I still haven't finished folding up all the foil.

Randy Scuffle
Your patient

Belmont hot-dog storm,
Everyone runs for shelter:
Art Institute calls

Dr. Anderson,

The bomb shelter is the best. There is a vent that goes up between some bushes and there is room to cook and sleep and everything. It's not so dusty either since I wiped it out. I don't think my mom knows how big this place is. This is way bigger than my bedroom in the house.

I have already begun setting up the table for some experiments on the shoes I want to make for my mom, but I can't remember what size shoes she wears. If I make them too big she will get mad or her feet will fall out of them. If I make them too small she will split the bologna trying to put them on. The good part though is that I can always adjust them without having to put them on the shoe stretching machine in the garage. I don't think the bologna could hold up to the pressure without ending up on the walls or down the neck of my shirt, like that time with the butter.

Please send more buckets and lots of batteries for my flashlight. I think they are D batteries. There is an extra door down here that I want to check out but it is locked with a combination and I have to work on that. I am going to employ the Feynman method for cracking the lock. It worked on that weird locker behind the CTA garage that used to be on Clark street. That is now condominiums, by the way, in case you are looking for one, although if you miss out on that you will probably still be able to get one in the neighborhood.

I think I read somewhere that everything on the North side is going to become a condominium. Personally I hope they turn the grocery store on Southport into condominiums because then the people who work there won't be so unhappy any more. It must be a terrible place to work because all they do while you're checking out is talk about their unions and who is going to take a break next. I think they are mainly unhappy because they have to work in the one store that carries produce that rots before it ripens. It must hurt their pride or something. I have to go now. Don't forget the batteries please.

Thank you,

Randy, your Chicago patient

Dr. Anderson,

This morning I became more intrigued by the door with the lock. I noticed there was a cool breeze coming from one of the edges. I started working on the lock and you'll be happy to know I figured out the combination.

Even more interesting though was the fact that when I opened it up it wasn't a closet filled with more beans or toilet paper like I expected. It wasn't disappointing like when you get to summer camp and instead of all the fun stuff you think you're going to be doing because of the images the brochures put in your mind, you get fed Spanish rice without hot dog chunks, you can only do archery once the whole time at camp, and someone steals your plaster bust of George Washington before you even get it out of the rubber mold. I think that's one reason I like to work in meat. People think twice about stealing it from you if it has already been carved to resemble a surprised beaver (or Brad Pitt).

I still think Donald Trump™ deserves a chance to live forever by the way, and perhaps he and Ryan Seacrest™ (whose name still sounds like a refreshing aftershave) should be the first to try the Sea Monkey™ treatments. Then, when people accuse Donald Trump™ of saying something troubling, he can defend his mental honor and reputation by describing how he is undergoing Sea Monkey™ treatments, and that the customized colony in his head is actually working to help him live forever. I think people would like to hear that.

Anyway, I thought you should know that behind the door is actually a tunnel. I don't know where it leads. I am going to find out tomorrow. Thanks again for all the D batteries, Dr. Anderson. I'll let you know what I find. And if my mom gets weird again, please tell her I'm okay.

Thank you,

Randy Scuffle, Chicago patient

END

Email: randy@randyscuffle.com
Twitter: @RandyScuffle
Facebook: Randy Scuffle